DIVINE

RETURN

Death Is Never The End

Jeff Walton

Divine Return: Death Is Never The End by Jeff Walton
© 2020 Jeff Walton. All rights reserved.
Printed in the USA.

ISBN: 978-0-9974334-3-2 (Paperback)
ISBN: 978-0-9974334-4-9 (Kindle)
ISBN: 978-0-9974334-5-6 (Hardcover)

LCCN: 2020910559

Sunbrook Publishing
PO Box 730
St. Augustine, FL 32085
www.JeffWaltonBooks.com
JeffWaltonBooks@gmail.com

Book Cover Design: Rik Feeney / www.RickFeeney.com
Cover: *Path to Light* by rolffimages / stock.adobe.com

DIVINE RETURN picks up where Walton's multiple-award-winning *FINAL DEPARTURE* left off.

Can a day of death become the start of a new life?

Dedication

To my loving Creator, Father God; to my King, Jesus Christ; and to my Companion, the Holy Spirit. This book would not have been possible without you.

Acknowledgments

My profound gratitude goes to the people who made *Divine Return* possible.

First, to the team of professionals that produced *Final Departure* and returned to apply their superior skills to *Divine Return*. Nancy Quatrano took the *Divine Return* manuscript and shaped it with skill through her expert content editing. Beth Mansbridge polished the final manuscript with care and precision during her copyediting. Rik Feeney, cover and book designer, took the words and expertly converted them into a finished product wrapped in a cover that conveys the book's inner message.

Chief Brian Lee and Detective Jose Jimenez, of the St. Johns County Sheriff's Office, shared important technical information on the local procedures their team of law enforcement professionals uses to process crime scenes.

Theri Boggess provided valuable insights into the topic of satanic ritual abuse and the underlying occult practices and beliefs that spur the dark arts.

Bryan Melvin, author of *A Land Unknown*: *Hell's Dominion*, and a near-death-experience witness, supplied critical firsthand information on what lies beyond life for some.

And to my wife Tess, who put up with my long hours and many months cloistered in my office while I researched and wrote. Thank you for your love and patience.

Contents

Did you know?

FACT:

Every day, approximately 774 people undergo a near-death experience in the United States.

FACT:

According to the National Center for Missing and Exploited Children, more than 400,000 children are reported missing each year in the United States.

FACT:

At least 163,500 people, or about 1/2% of the United States population, suffer from dissociative identity disorder, also known as multiple personality disorder. Some studies estimate as many as 654,000 are afflicted.

Chapter 1
Confirmation

Back from the dead? Fourteen minutes with no pulse or respiration—he should be a drooling vegetable. I can't believe he's alive!

Dan Lucas made his way to the front door of the modest single-story Florida rambler, not sure of who or what to expect when the door opened. The iron-stained concrete pavers in the front yard walkway were still wet from overnight watering, and the strong smell of sulfur from the well water singed his nostrils.

His mind was a kaleidoscope of images and memories fading in and out of his consciousness. *Who gets a phone call from a dead man?* After more than a year of assuming his new acquaintance, Professor Ben Chernick, had died of a heart attack in a Charlotte, North Carolina, hospital, Dan was now steps away from seeing the man who had amazingly come back to life. Dan's former US Naval Criminal Investigative Service (NCIS) career of dealing with murder and mayhem had not prepared him for this moment. Ben's shocking call on Christmas Day to announce he was still alive had turned Dan's world upside down. He was about to reunite with a man who was a walking miracle.

Dan rang the doorbell near the cream-colored front doorway and waited patiently in the early May morning. A gentle Atlantic Ocean breeze bathed his face with a moist warmth and momentarily melted his apprehension. He felt a mixture of excitement and anxiety as he studied the dimly lit doorbell button that had yellowed from the intense Florida sunlight. His mind began to drift. *Maybe he'll laugh at me with his sarcastic wheeze, or maybe this is all an elaborate hoax .... There you go again—where's your faith? You know this is real. You've been studying this phenomenon for years.* Dan heard the yipping of a small dog and a muffled command for the dog to be still.

He had been rehearsing this moment during his seventy-minute drive from Jacksonville, Florida, to Palm Coast—a trip he'd been anticipating for months. He felt the same inquisitiveness today that he used to feel before a major interrogation in an NCIS criminal case.

Ben, his former fellow airline traveler and would-be Christian convert, had survived his extraordinary ordeal at the Charlotte Douglas International Airport and was now waiting in the flesh to tell Dan all about it. The two had spent nearly twelve hours trapped in an ice-encrusted terminal, trading barbs and jabs in between serious discussions about life, death, God, and the Bible. In stages, Dan had laid out his case for faith in Christ—building a case based on evidence—often leaving Ben stammering for words before resorting to his trademark sarcasm and cynical appeals to human reason. But Ben's sudden death had brought the overnight ordeal to a crushing end.

The smiling face and warm brown eyes of Ruth Williams, Ben's daughter, greeted Dan as she welcomed him into a small foyer. He embraced Ruth with a heartfelt hug, and a flood of memories poured into his mind. He relived the moment when she woke him from a deep sleep in the Mercy Medical Center room in Charlotte, where Ben had been admitted that fateful morning. Although she and her father had been estranged for more than a decade, she'd eagerly flown to Charlotte to be at Ben's hospital bedside. Dan had called her from the back of an ambulance while medics worked to revive Ben after his second heart attack. Several hours after Ruth's arrival, Ben had suffered a third coronary—a fatal one. Remarkably, he spontaneously revived fourteen minutes after having been declared dead by an attending physician.

Dan snapped out of his reverie when an unbelievably slim and trim Ben Chernick strode into the room, his face beaming a wide smile. Here was a changed man. The sixty-two-year-old academician, dressed in his trademark khakis and blue polo shirt, embraced Dan with surprising strength. Then he motioned for Dan to follow him through the family room.

"It's about time you got here," Ben said, though his grin betrayed his faux irritation. "I call you up and it takes you five months to make it down?"

Dan laughed, delighted that Ben was alive to tease him. "You haven't changed a bit, Ben! Yeah, we had to go up north and help our daughter and her three kids pack out while her husband reported to his new Air Force duty station early. Family comes first, these days."

"You've got your priorities straight, my friend. Come this way. You're a sight for sore eyes."

***

Corporal Felton checked for a pulse with his gloved hand, and then stood up while staring at the child's lifeless body. He was second to arrive on the scene, after Deputy Pearce. Felton had seen scores of bodies at crime scenes throughout the county over the years, but this one was different. He took a deep breath and wiped the early morning Florida humidity off his forehead with his right forearm.

"Who called this in?"

"A couple of guys who came back here to hunt wild pigs. One of the dogs started barking and pulled his owner toward the body." Deputy Pearce glanced at his notepad. "The call came in at seven thirty-two this morning."

Corporal Felton shifted his gaze from the deputy, back to the victim. "From the condition of the body, I'd say she was dumped here within the last twenty-four hours. Who else from Major Crimes has been notified?"

"The shift supervisor's on his way and so is Walker."

"Don't touch anything—you know how Walker is. We don't want him to get his panties in a wad, do we?"

The St. Johns County Sheriff's deputy laughed and shook his head knowingly. "Don't worry, I won't touch a thing!"

"Let's put some tape around the area and make sure no one gets near the body. I'll wait for Walker and the crime scene techs."

***

Ben handed Dan a large mug of steaming coffee and opened a French door that led to a sizeable screened-in back porch. He ushered him toward a white wicker lounge chair with thick maroon cushions. The porch was tastefully decorated with a tropical-themed outdoor living room set. Several painted ceramic pots with assorted plants lined the inside perimeter of the screened enclosure.

"I've been relishing this moment for months," Ben announced as he took a seat in an adjoining chair. He sipped his coffee. *This man saved my life! I am so glad he's here!*

"I still can't get over what happened last year," Dan said. "When Ruth called and told me you were dead, I mentally shut down. Never in a million years did I ever expect you could survive. Then, when you called me last Christmas, I was positive it was a sick prank. I knew there was no way you could be alive."

He set his coffee mug down on the wicker coffee table in front of him. "I've thought about our night together in the airport a thousand times and still can't believe what happened. You were dead, Ben, more than once! I watched you go into cardiac arrest on the airport floor and then I saw you flatline in the ambulance."

"Oh, I was dead," Ben replied. "Physically—at least for a few minutes. But before we get into what happened to me, I want to know how you've been. You have no idea how impressed I was with your ability to present your case for Christianity and argue against my reason with logic of your own. A man with your talents should be changing the world."

"I've been trying," Dan confided. "After I got home from Charlotte, I wanted to put your death behind me. I immersed myself in my writing and tried to block everything else out. I finished the book, but I paid a price."

"How so?" Ben asked. "You convinced me you had it all together. The perfect family man guided by God."

"But human, too," Dan said. "Like I did in my old career, I focused too much on getting the book written, and I ignored my family. Connie did all the work helping Sienna, our youngest daughter, with our new granddaughter, who was born the day you died—and came back. I reverted into a workaholic and shut everything and everyone else out. I felt driven to get my message into print so I could share it with the world."

"Are you on the outs with your wife? You were the one giving me advice on loving others and protecting and nurturing our children. Now you're saying you were selfish and put yourself first. I'm surprised," Ben said, his brow furrowed.

"Oh, I snapped out of it after I finished the final draft of my manuscript. Connie got my attention the way she always does—with honesty wrapped in humor and grace. She pointed out the cold, hard truth. I was more worried about what others would think about my book than the feelings of my family. She has a way with words that cut, but then heal. I realized I was being selfish. I handed my manuscript off to my editor and centered my attention on being a husband, father, and grandfather again. Don't worry, I'm back on track." Dan paused for a second and sharpened his gaze on Ben's face. "The big question is … how did you die and come back to life?"

Ben shifted in his chair and leaned toward Dan. "I was dead, all right, but not dead in the way we think."

"How so?" Dan asked. "After I left the hospital, Ruth called while I was boarding my flight home. She told me you'd died. I thought you were gone for good."

"I was not on this earth during those fourteen minutes, Dan," Ben stated. *Now I'm the one who has to make him believe. ...* "That's why I wanted you to come here so we could talk. You were right, my friend. Near-death experiences are real! Now I need to find a way to convince people that what I experienced actually happened. Everyone has to know what's at stake before it's too late. It was almost too late for me, but your sermons saved me in more ways than one."

"So you *did* have one!" Dan nearly shouted.

"I didn't have one, I had *three*!" Ben replied, almost breathless. "Some of the details come back to me out of order, but I remember having the first one while I was still in the airport. Not sure where I was, exactly, but I remember being on my back, in great pain, and looking up at you and the crowd around me, and an older gentleman kneeling beside me."

"He was a doctor who came to help after an announcement for medical assistance was made over the airport's PA system," Dan said. "You went into cardiac arrest, and he began CPR."

"That's when it happened the first time," Ben announced. He paused and his posture stiffened when the memory came back. "In seconds, I found myself speeding through a black tunnel and landing in a black cavernous space that had to have been a thousand degrees—yet I still had a body and was alive. I should have been incinerated in seconds. I could smell horrific odors and heard millions of deafening screams. The smells were so bad I could taste them. But I was alive—more alive than I am now. I could sense everything in sort of a multidimensional way. Sounds had odors, and odors had a physical quality to them. It was pitch-black, but I could sense the presence of something near me. I was terrified, Dan. Words can't express what I experienced. The darkness had a physical quality to it, too. I could sense, taste, and feel it. It was evil in a solidified form. I felt an incredible sense of doom, and then I suddenly popped back into my body. The gentleman was kneeling next to me when I came back."

"That's when your heart starting beating again! I remember you were agitated. Now I understand why," Dan said.

"The rest of my recall of that morning is sort of fragmented. I remember being in a van, and that's when I had the second one. The *really* bad one! I can still feel the terror." Ben wiped his brow with his handkerchief and shut his eyes momentarily.

"We were in the ambulance then," Dan said. "I was riding with you and the EMT crew, and after they got you hooked up to their equipment and we were headed to the hospital, you flatlined. They did CPR and had to use a defibrillator since, when your heartbeat came back, it was wildly erratic."

"That's when I found myself in a small pit with flames coming up out of a void at the bottom, but I sensed the pit went much deeper, somehow," Ben said. "I clung to the sides since I couldn't climb out. Some sort of creature was pacing near the pit. I knew the thing would attack me if I tried to climb out. I could feel its stare through the dark. The flames felt like a million razor blades slicing through my body. The place was pitch-black except for the light from the flames. The light wasn't a normal light, though. It didn't travel very far. The flames were almost black and seemed to be alive. Somehow, I could sense there were other pits with people in them all around me, but I was so preoccupied with my own pain and horror, I didn't try to look around. Agony doesn't begin to describe it. I simultaneously felt stark terror and extreme hopelessness. I knew I was in a place I'd never get out of. The worst part was I knew I deserved to be there. The experience seemed like it took days, but I later learned I was flatlined for less than a minute or two. Once my condition stabilized and I could think clearly again, I realized your theories about hell were true. Words can't describe the horror of that place. I'll never forget it."

Ben put his face in his hands and slumped forward. He felt the complete helplessness all over again, even after all this time. But he had to help Dan know, without a doubt, that he'd been right about hell and the price for not believing. After more than a minute of silence, he looked up slowly with tears in his eyes, appreciating Dan's respectful quietness.

"Not my theories—remember, Ben? It's the fine research of others I've tapped into, and now you can add to it. Remember how I explained hellish NDEs confirm what's written in the Bible?" Dan paused for a moment, studying his friend's facial expression. "Now I know why you were so apoplectic when you were revived in the ambulance. You were screaming into your oxygen mask."

"Yes! I went from flames to the back of the ambulance in an instant. I was still reacting to the pain when I came to. Horror doesn't come close to describing my emotions then. I was terrified I'd end up back there. I've only recently been able to talk about it." *And not to many people.*

Dan was fascinated. "Have you told Ruth and Tim?"

"I have, but like you warned me, they say they believe me, but I can tell they're only patronizing me. They think I'm a sick old man who had a medical trauma that produced hallucinations. I'm not going to keep trying to convince them my experiences were real. I have more important things to do. My mission became clear during my third NDE. I have to tell the world that everything I used to believe was a lie."

Chapter 2
Gathering Storm

The young man adjusted the rearview mirror in his faded dark blue green Saturn after coming to a stop at a railroad crossing. The high-mileage sedan showed its years of hard driving and lack of maintenance, with its pulsating brake pedal and rough idle. He scanned the cars behind him for signs of something out of place. *They have my plate number and know my car.*

The deep vibration of an approaching freight train radiated through the car's frame and up into the seats. He readjusted his gaze to the car stopped in front of him while the clinking of a warning bell sounded as the crossing barriers came down. When he looked to the right of the car in front, he froze. The sight of the blinking red barrier warning lights triggered grinding fear and gut-wrenching horror. Beads of sweat formed on his forehead. His eyelids fluttered, and he flinched, expecting the searing pain of a cattle prod. *Not again!* Closing his eyes, he slumped forward against the steering wheel. He stayed motionless while the train rumbled by and the gates opened. The loud honking behind him snapped his main personality back, and he accelerated forward while wrestling to compose himself.

***

Detective Walker pulled up in his unmarked Ford cruiser and parked next to a half-dozen patrol cars. He made his way through the sand pines, into a clearing in the woods where the initial responders were standing outside of the taped-off crime scene.

"Medical examiner investigators called yet?"

"They'll be here in five."

"Who found the body?"

"Those guys over there by my car," Corporal Felton said. "They came back in here to hunt feral pigs with bows and found the body about two hours ago. Their story seems legit."

"I'll be the judge of that. They got IDs?"

"Yep."

Detective Walker proceeded cautiously on the sandy turf dotted with clumps of weeds, careful not to disturb anything. When the child's small frame came into view, the detective suppressed his urge to gag. A four- or five-year-old female body, completely disrobed, with blood-caked brown hair, was on her back. Her light green eyes were still open in a fixed gaze. A series of black *X*s were drawn on her chest and torso. Each *X* was over a corresponding vital organ, and all but one were sites of multiple puncture wounds. Some appeared superficial, and others appeared to be deeper and most likely fatal.

Why are there stab wounds on all of the Xs *but one?* Holding his revulsion in check, Walker examined the body for more possible clues. Her thin arms were carefully positioned next to her body. He maneuvered to look closer and saw several fresh burns on her arms, chest, and legs. Abrasions and bruising around her wrists were plainly visible. Walker closed his eyes and fought nausea while straightening up. The sickness in the pit of his stomach shot through his body and caused him to momentarily lose his balance. He caught himself from stumbling.

"What kind of sick bastard would do this to a child! I want a deputy posted to keep the area secure. Crime scene techs on their way?"

"They're finishing up the suicide at the beach. Should be here by ten thirty."

"I don't want anyone near the body. Is that clear?"

***

Dan waited for Ben to continue his story. Retelling was obviously painful for his friend. He couldn't imagine what the actual experience must have been like.

Ben took a sip of his coffee and stared straight at Dan. "The third NDE is what I need to tell you about—the reason I asked you to come down. I remember bits and pieces of being in the hospital and being moved from room to room," he said. "First, what do you remember?"

Dan leaned back in the wicker chair while reliving the tense morning when he'd fought exhaustion and despair following the historic ice storm. He rested his head against the chair's back, gazed at the ceiling, and gathered his thoughts.

"We got to the Carolinas Mercy Medical Center around seven, right after the city reopened the roads in Charlotte. Everything was still covered in ice. The medical staff had you in ICU for about an hour and then transferred you to a room in the heart center before your cardiac cath. I remember seeing a look of fear in your face, but I thought it was a result of your heart attacks," Dan said.

"Yeah, Ruth told me the same thing. I vaguely remember being lightly sedated for the cardiac catheterization, but kept dozing off. I remember waking up when they brought me back to my room, where Ruth was waiting—but you weren't there. I was shocked to see Ruth, but at the same time she brought me great comfort. I couldn't think clearly, so I wasn't able to tell her that I had been on my way to visit her. I explained everything later."

"That's when I left the hospital to go catch my plane home," Dan said. "Ruth was with you, so I thought you'd be okay."

"Deserting your friend, huh?" Ben had a good-natured laugh as he put his coffee mug down. Then his expression sobered. "That's when it happened." Ben shifted in his chair and leaned toward Dan. He spoke in a near whisper. "After my cardiac catheterization, they brought me back to my room. I remember Ruth sitting in a chair, looking at me while I was still groggy. I remember feeling like an elephant had sat on my chest, and the next thing I knew I flew out of my body, into a dark tunnel again. Oh, the terrible screams I heard and the putrid odors I smelled while I shot through it! I landed in a medieval cell. The walls were roughhewn stone, but it had metal bars that fitted over irregularly-shaped windows and some sort of metal door. I could see out of the windows into other cells that were next to mine on either side.

"I watched a man—I assumed it was a man—being lowered by chains around his ankles, into the adjoining cell. He didn't have any skin, only some sinewy material over his bones. He had eyes but no eyelids, and he frantically looked around in terror as he hung upside down. The door to his cell opened, and a huge, demon-like creature stomped in and stuck clawlike fingers into his body and dug down and out. It ripped this person's chest cavity open as the person writhed in pain and screamed an awful guttural sound. Not a drop of blood came out." Ben stopped, took a deep breath, and continued in a shaky voice.

"The person survived the attack, somehow. He shook his head violently in pain, and within seconds the sinewy material grew back over his bones. I could see it growing almost instantly. The demon left the cell while the person hung there." Ben scrubbed his face with his handkerchief and paused.

Though his own heart was pounding hard and fast while hearing Ben's words, Dan could see that Ben was reliving the terror all over again. "Do you want to take a break?"

Ben shook his head. "No, this will never get any easier. I can still feel the terror like I'm there. But I need to get to the important part. You're the one person who'll understand what happened to me."

"You could see all this from your cell window?" Dan asked. He was in a near state of mild shock while listening to Ben's harrowing story.

"Yeah, it was nearly pitch-black, but there was a flickering light in the background that was bright enough for me to see my surroundings. It was a pale orange light. I suddenly remembered you, Dan, and all of your words poured back into my mind. I remembered how you said Christ deliberately died on the cross in our place, to pay for our sins on earth so that no one had to go to hell. I was racking my brain, asking myself, 'What do I have to do, what do I have to do?' I can't tell you the fear and hopelessness I felt. I was screaming at myself, 'What do I do!' " Ben stopped again and swallowed hard.

With a grimace, he focused on Dan. "Then I felt chains around my ankles. My cell door opened by itself, and I was being dragged by the chains along the rough rock path. I felt terror beyond description. As I was being pulled along, the light got brighter and I could hear a loud sound like a jet engine. I lifted my head and saw that I was being dragged straight toward a pulsating orange light. I could feel tremendous heat."

Ben stopped and put his hands over his face, and remained silent for a moment. After he regained his composure, he continued in a whisper. "I was being dragged toward a pit of flames. While I was screaming, I kept trying to remember what you told me. The chains pulled me down into a slippery substance like grease that was on fire, and the flames and searing agony engulfed me. I can't describe the pain. Words can't do it justice." He stopped again and swallowed hard.

"While my body was being reduced to a charred cadaver, I heard myself scream, 'Help me, Jesus! Help me, Jesus!' " Ben faced the sky and said, "Through the flames I saw two huge bluish-white hands reach into the flames and pull me out. I was lifted into the air and immediately the burning stopped. I felt peace and calm as I floated up over that enormous pit of fire. It must have been several miles wide. I could see other people bobbing up and down in the burning liquid. All I know is I was being lifted by those huge luminous hands, and the next thing I know is I realize those hands were connected to a person wearing a white robe."

Ben turned, made eye contact with Dan, and swallowed hard. "A brilliant white light blinded me, so I couldn't see the person's face, but I could hear his thoughts." The older man's eyes were wide and his voice was rising. "I heard him think, *I have been waiting for you to call my name.* I instantly knew it was Jesus Christ. He saved me."

Ben covered his face with his hands and convulsed into sobs. He forced himself to continue. "The love I felt … was so intense … and I was so ashamed! … I didn't deserve … to be pulled out of that place … but Jesus felt such a strong love for me. … I felt like a child being rescued by a parent."

Dan nodded to him and, not wanting to break Ben's momentum, stayed in his chair.

After sobbing for several minutes, Ben breathed slowly and deeply. He wiped the tears from his eyes with a forearm and focused on Dan.

"We floated upward," said Ben, "and Christ began to speak to me with thoughts. His sentences were short, concise. His thoughts cascaded into my mind like bursts of information. I could hear them clearly. I'll never forget the central message he gave me. *I have brought you from this place so that you may tell others what you have seen. You have spent your life denying that I exist. Now you know the truth. You have served yourself, now serve me. It is not yet your time. Go in peace.*

"The next thing I knew, I was back in my body. Ruth screamed when I sat straight up in the hospital bed. They were getting ready to wheel me down to the morgue. I sure gave that orderly a shock when I pulled off the sheet covering my face. All hell broke loose then—pardon the pun. Doctors came running into the room to examine me. They were confused. One doctor was irate. He said he'd pronounced me dead and there I was. Everyone was speechless.

They kept me overnight to run a whole battery of tests, but once they decided I was perfectly fine, they released me.

"We went back to the airport to catch a flight to Jacksonville, and Ruth forgot her cell phone in the ladies' room there. That's why I didn't call you for months. I didn't have your number, and Ruth never wrote it down. Since you were a former spook, I couldn't find a trace of you on the net. I had to cull through every online church directory in the Jacksonville area until I finally found your number." A look of satisfaction settled on Ben's face.

Dan was euphoric. Here in front of him sat his friend, alive and well. And even more importantly, his friend had been to hell and with Jesus, too. Now Dan had a trusted witness who could confirm all the research material he had studied.

"You're absolutely positive this happened?"

"I've never been surer of anything in my life. Somehow, I've got to convince others what happened to me was real, and that the stakes for all of us are so much higher than anyone could imagine. I can't do it alone, though, Dan. I need you. I need your help. You have to help me make this happen."

**

Detective Walker strode back to his car with the image of the young child's blood-caked hair still firmly planted in his mind's eye. The girl reminded him of his own daughter, Willow. Nearly numb, he swung open the door of his Ford Taurus, started the engine, and sat in the air conditioning as he fought to control his emotions. *I'm gonna find the animal who did this ... he'll pay. ... I've gotta get out of this job. I can't take this anymore. Not when a kid's involved.*

The normally stoic Florida State grad fought back tears while he sat in his car, waiting for the medical examiner to arrive. Based on his years of experience he knew the homicide case would be stressful and challenging, but had no idea the child's death was linked to something much more sinister.

**

"Let's face it, Tim, attendance is down and expenses are going up. We can't continue to operate at a deficit and keep our doors open," said Carl James, the heavyset church council chairman. "We've already made every cut we can make, and we even postponed hiring a second youth ministry leader."

Tim Williams, pastor of Radiant Love Church, met Carl's gaze. Their church was an independent place of worship without a sponsoring denomination to supplement its operating expenses. The air in the church office was stuffy and uncomfortably warm. An overworked window air conditioner hummed in the background.

Tim leaned back in his worn black vinyl office chair and gazed at the bisque acoustic ceiling tiles while he collected his thoughts. Radiant Love Church was his brainchild and labor of love. After marrying Ruth Chernick, Ben's daughter, the couple had moved to Palm Coast, Florida, where Tim had vowed to start a church. He had nearly given up on his dream when he stumbled upon a vacant church building that needed only minor repairs. Together with the help of a few fellow believers, he was able to refurbish the dated structure and assume the mortgage. Now, all he had worked for was in jeopardy.

"We've got to find a way to boost attendance and offering levels—especially at the contemporary service. That used to be our best attended service," Carl stated. "Why don't you have your father-in-law come in and tell about his back-to-life experience? Maybe you can do a sermon series as a spin-off. We could do an article in the paper and draw in the curious."

Tim had his doubts. He respected Ben, but wasn't comfortable with preaching about a phenomenon that some had said was the work of the devil. To his mind, NDEs were unbiblical; he wasn't ready to preach about something so controversial and risk losing even more worshippers. "Not a bad idea … but maybe something else. Let me think about it," Tim said.

He was desperate to save his dream. Initially the church had grown and attendance continued to make gains, but as families grew older, the teens and young adults stopped attending, and soon their parents became less frequent attendees too. Tim was at a loss to explain their lack of faith and commitment. His sermons had been theologically sound. After all, he'd been an honor student in seminary after he and Ruth had married, and he had been thoroughly prepared to carry the message of hope and Jesus Christ to the new generations—or so he thought. He made sure his sermons were a message of faith and inspiration, but something was missing. *Why can't I connect with the younger generation? Are they really so different from me?*

***

Detective Charlie Walker squatted next to the young girl's body and pushed away a clump of weeds to allow the crime scene technician a clear view of the immediate death scene. The din of insects and birds chirping in the wooded area filled his ears while waves of humid heat pulsed from the Northeast Florida turf. Walker had long since learned to tune out all distractions to focus on the task at hand.

Crime Scene Technician Turner, from the St. Johns County Sheriff's Office, had arrived at the scene a half hour after receiving Detective Walker's call. Turner, a stout man in his mid-forties, slipped on a pair of latex exam gloves and carefully began to check near the body for anything that might be of evidentiary value. After making some notes on a pad, he shined his bullet flashlight on some of the wounds on the child's body to get a better grasp as to the possible cause of death. The light caught the faint outline of a curved line that had been traced in the sandy soil around the body. Turner stood and noticed the curved line was part of a complete circle that was now visible in the late morning sun.

"Did you see this? Someone drew a circle around the body. It looks fresh." Without waiting for a response, Turner made a note and added the date and his name to the top of the page. From his left jacket pocket he pulled out a camera and took a photo.

Walker felt a flush of indignation and embarrassment for missing such an obvious piece of potential evidence.

This was put here. Now I have to figure out why.

Chapter 3
Mounting Pressure

Observing the doctor in front of him, Ben wondered what the examination would show. He'd almost cancelled this appointment because he thought it would be a waste of time.

"Deep breath."

Dr. Richard Shapiro held his brushed steel stethoscope in his tanned hands against Ben Chernick's chest, listening intently to his lungs. The cardiologist remained still as he strained to hear signs of congestion and restriction. His heavily starched white lab coat and gold-rimmed glasses gave the silver-haired doctor a distinguished demeanor.

"Unbelievably clear for a man with chronic emphysema," he said, taking a step back. "Your heart also sounds fine. EKG was normal, as was your bloodwork. If I didn't know better, I'd say I was examining someone who brought in the wrong chart. Remarkable for a man who had three myocardial infarctions and complete cardiac arrest for fourteen minutes."

"You don't know the half of it, Doc," Ben stated while glancing at the floor. He knew this moment was coming. "My recovery isn't something you'd read about in your medical journals. I had a little help."

The doctor's eyebrows jumped sharply. "Is that so? Your chart says you had a spontaneous resuscitation after being declared dead. An amazing recovery indeed. Who helped you?"

"Are you familiar with near-death experiences?"

"Can't say that I am. I understand some studies have been done on the subject, but I'm not convinced. Are you saying you had one?" He made some notes in Ben's chart.

"I am. I didn't have one NDE, Doc, I had three. I left my body, went to hell, and I was saved by Jesus Christ." The instant Ben blurted out his confession, he regretted it. *Oh boy, here we go.*

Dr. Shapiro stopped writing and visibly stiffened.

After a moment, his large brown eyes held Ben's attention. "The brain is a complex organ, Mr. Chernick. I've been studying medicine for over forty years, and I'm still learning. You underwent extreme trauma—trauma that would have permanently incapacitated or killed most people. The severe shock you experienced overloaded your thought processes. I know you think something extraordinary happened, but there is no medical evidence to support your beliefs. The brain is an incredibly resourceful organ that can create thoughts or provide a mental escape to help you cope under extreme circumstances."

"Doc, you're not listening," Ben said, waving his hands. "I didn't have a bad dream. I didn't hallucinate. I had the most vivid experiences of my life. I know it's hard to believe. I didn't believe in NDEs either, until I found out for myself they're real. Before my heart attacks, I was a stone-cold atheist. You couldn't get me near a church or synagogue. But it happened. It happened to me and I know it was real. I know God is real and so is Jesus Christ. He's as real as you and me."

Dr. Shapiro walked over to a bookcase behind his desk and picked up a gilded picture frame. The faded and slightly crumpled black-and-white photo of a young woman dressed in an elegant gown reminded Ben of photos he had seen of his paternal grandmother.

"This is a photograph of my late mother, Rosetta. She was gassed in Auschwitz by the Nazis. Mr. Chernick, if a God exists, as you claim he does, where was he when they marched my dear mother into the gas chamber? You have a great God of love? I don't think so."

"I know, I know." Ben groaned, searching for words to answer the doctor's brutally honest point. "I used to feel the same way. But you've got it wrong, Doc. As incredible as it sounds, I was in his presence and I can tell you he is pure love. A love so intense a mere mortal couldn't stand it. I don't know how to answer you, but I know there's an answer. I've spent my entire life hiding from God, but he found me. I know there are answers, and when I get them, you'll be the first to know."

"Mr. Chernick, I received my answer many years ago, and I've seen nothing to change my mind. Besides, we're talking about your medical condition and the facts contained in your record—not about philosophy."

Ben felt his anger rising. "Why is it that when you professionals encounter something new that breaks currently accepted paradigms, you always fall back on what you think you know? Why can't you accept new information and consider it to be possible?"

Dr. Shapiro folded his stethoscope neatly and placed it on his exam room desk. He quietly gazed out the window. After several moments of silence, he began to speak while still facing away from Ben. "I have some very good friends in psychiatry. Would you like me to make a referral? Sometimes it's good to talk over things that are troubling you. I've had several patients who needed counseling after traumatic cardiac events. I think it would do you some good."

Ben was headed out the door before the cardiologist finished talking.

"Mr. Chernick!"

He kept moving.

"Mr. Chernick! Continue your medications. I want to see you back here in three months," Dr. Shapiro called loudly in a near pleading tone.

Ben slammed the office door shut behind him. *I knew no one would believe me.*

***

Dan pushed the handle on the elliptical trainer hard with his right hand one last time and slowly decelerated to a stop. He'd finished his standard ninety-minute workout and wiped his face with a towel. After dismounting, he went over to the biceps machine to chat with his friend.

One critical life lesson Dan had learned in his new life of writing and retirement was his need to spend some time around like-minded men. Men with the same intense background he had. He'd found what he was searching for in a St. Augustine gym, where he'd made a couple of good friends. Detective Charlie Walker fit neatly in the center of Dan's clearly established parameters—he was law enforcement, near retirement age, and a man of faith.

When Dan made eye contact with Charlie, who had met him to do a workout, he seemed listless and withdrawn.

"Rough week?" Dan asked as the detective finished his wipe-down of the chrome and vinyl-clad machine. Dan moved toward the end of a row of empty treadmills, and Charlie matched his steps.

"Yeah, you might say so. I think it's time to retire. You knew when it was time, didn't you?"

"Oh, I knew. When the thrill is gone and you start to see your organization go backward—then it's time to pull the plug." Anything in particular going on?"

"I had another long week, but one case has gotten under my skin. I can't get it out of my head."

Dan had been around Charlie long enough to know when something bothered him. They'd initially met at a Christian Business Leaders luncheon, when Dan joined several years earlier. Eager to make new friends after he and Connie and their daughters had moved to Jacksonville, Dan thought the leadership group would be a good way to meet people.

At first, Charlie was intrigued by Dan's NCIS background—an interest that led to an eventual friendship. They'd established a routine of meeting in the St. Augustine gym, where Dan continued his workouts to keep Father Time at bay.

Dan studied Charlie's face carefully before speaking. "Anything you want to talk about?"

"Did you do many homicides in NCIS?"

"I did a few early in my career, but some of my fellow agents did them all the time. Why?"

"I have one I can't figure out, and that's rare for me. This one is a child victim with some odd wound patterns. She was found in the woods with a circle drawn in the dirt around her body. I've never seen symbols planted at a death scene before. Maybe it's some sort of new gang or cult. Child homicides always get to me. I want to catch the scum who did it, but I don't know who or what I'm looking for."

"Want me to take a look at your case file?"

"I was hoping you'd ask. Can you come by the office tomorrow?"

"Sure can."

***

Tim's finger traced the words on his computer screen while he read out loud. "Fifty-nine percent of all youth who go to Sunday school as children stop going to church by their late teens. Children who attended Sunday school are more skeptical of the Bible than those who never attended any religious training as a child." He shook his head when he finished reading the results of the study he'd found during an internet search.

"Why would religious training turn kids away from God?"

Chapter 4
Pushback

Beads of sweat formed on the young man's forehead while he stared blankly ahead. The vivid images in his mind had stopped for the time being, and he could concentrate on navigating the road in front of him. At near dusk, he pulled up in front of a run-down two-story bungalow framed by scraggly live oaks, the contorted branches draped in Spanish moss. Unraked leaves littered the ground around the tree and clung to the mold-stained, brown-shingled roof.

The forlorn young man listlessly made his way through the unkempt yard, toward the stairway leading to the second-story apartment. He dreaded another night alone. With his keys clanging in the deadbolt, he felt the phone in his right-front pocket ring once and stop. It rang again two times and stopped, followed by three rings. He froze, feeling his mind go blank.

They found me ....

***

"My father-in-law says you wrote a Christian novel," announced Tim Williams. He was stirring his half lemonade and iced tea mixture with gusto, which produced several seconds of loud clinking sounds.

Waiting until he could be heard easily, Dan said, "That's right." He cut into the hot stromboli on his plate with a knife and fork. Strings of mozzarella cheese stretched like rubber bands from the plate when he lifted a still-connected piece with his hands and took a big bite while maintaining eye contact with Tim.

Tim had invited Dan to lunch to pick his brain and talk candidly, away from his wife, Ruth, and father-in-law, Ben. Tim wasn't as nearly interested in the food or the charming New York–style pizzeria and black-and-white celebrity photos hanging on the walls as he was for guidance. Tim managed to take a bite from his oversized slice of pizza with great difficulty. He gave a nod that said "Go on."

"I've finished writing it," Dan said, "but it hasn't been published yet. The hard part of the writing business is finding a publisher who's a good fit for me and my message. Also, one who's willing to take me on, warts and all." Dan allowed himself a sheepish grin. "Lots harder than people think. With today's digital technology, thousands of new books are published every week, and it's not easy to separate yourself from the pack and get picked up by a decent publisher. I'm still beating the bushes. In the meantime, I'm working on my second book."

"Same subject?" Tim asked. He struggled to hold the large slice of pepperoni-and-mushroom pizza. After failing to fold the large piece to take a bite, he relented and cut it into pieces.

"Yeah, Christian fiction," Dan replied. "To be truthful, it's more fact than fiction. It's what some people call an information novel. I feel called to write what I think is the truth about the Bible."

"What do you mean?"

"Some pastors try to shield their congregations from the actual contents of the Bible and focus on the compassion and love shown by Jesus Christ. I think that's misleading the worshippers. Teaching about the mercy of Christ and not the judgment we'll face is almost spiritual malpractice, in my opinion."

Tim straightened in his chair. Dan's words stung. *Ouch. He's describing me.* In an even tone, Tim said, "What's wrong with focusing on Christ's grace and mercy?"

"Nothing, if it's a balanced message. The problem with focusing only on Christ's love is that it gives the impression that he has limitless compassion for all mankind and never administers judgment. Everyone gets into heaven regardless of whether or not they've humbled themselves and repented. The hyper-grace message distorts the truth of the Scriptures and leads people astray. You heard the eyewitness account of your own father-in-law. Hell is real and full of real people. Ignoring God and expecting to be admitted into heaven because they think he's a big softie will be the biggest mistake anyone could ever make. The eternal consequences are beyond our ability to comprehend. I feel a duty to get the truth out, and so does Ben."

Tim shifted in his seat, uncomfortable with the conversation. It hit too close to home. Dan was right, of course, but Tim didn't want to gamble with the topics that might scare people away. People were leaving the church in droves these days, even with sanitized and carefully worded messages.

"Dan, you're right, but most people aren't ready for a full shot of the truth. My attendance is going down, and the last thing I can afford to do right now is chase people away with a message of fire and brimstone."

"Start by building a foundation on the truth of the Old Testament. You don't need to zero in on hell and sin," Dan said with a slight shrug. "Start by teaching the truths of the Scriptures and how they relate to the natural world we live in today."

"I think that would bore people. No one wants to hear about Shadrach, Meshach, and Abednego. No one cares about the Jews being lost in the wilderness for forty years or the walls of Jericho tumbling down. They're old stories that put people to sleep."

"What about giants and half-human, half-angel hybrids? And animal-human crossbreeds. Do you think those biblical accounts would attract people?"

Tim frowned and cocked his head. "Giants and human-angel hybrids? Come on, Dan, that's not in the Bible."

"Oh, yes it is. The Bible is full of the most unbelievable information that makes science fiction look like a child's bedtime story. The Scriptures clearly document angels descending on earth, having intimate relations with human females, and producing a race of evil giant offspring. How's that for an attention getter? I can show you in black and white."

"I've never heard anyone teach about angels coming to earth and producing giants. Must have missed those lectures in seminary. Are you sure?"

"As sure as I know I'm sitting here with you. I'll tell you what, Tim. I'll pull together some reference material and come back down here and lay it all out. I'm sure Ben wouldn't mind if I made another trip down to visit. I need to sit down with him, anyway, and do a formal interview for my next book. We only scratched the surface the other day."

"You really believe he died and went to hell? I mean, Ruth and I respect Ben and admire him for his strength, but don't you think he could have hallucinated his experience while he was under incredible stress?"

Dan shook his head. "Not at all. His experiences fit the near-death-experience pattern perfectly. When I come back with the documentation on the angel-hybrids, I'll also bring some info on NDEs. When we're done, I'm positive you'll believe Ben."

"I hope you're right. Ruth and I were beginning to believe Ben was losing his mind. We were thinking of getting him some mental health counseling. You know, Ruth has a Ph.D., and she has some friends who are psychologists. We'll hold off until we hear back from you."

Dan nodded, and Tim wondered what in the world he'd gotten himself into.

***

Ben slid into the back row at Temple East Synagogue of Palm Coast and picked up a smoothly-worn leather prayer book from the seat. He was one of the first arrivals at the Jewish house of worship for the seven fifteen Friday night Shabbat service. The modest yet tastefully appointed worship room reminded Ben of a synagogue he and his parents had attended in Philadelphia when he was a child. The warm dark wood cabinetry and furniture pieces throughout the moderately large worship area, with its high-vaulted ceiling, gave the room an authentic and dignified atmosphere. While clutching the hardbound book with sweaty hands, an uneasiness gripped him as others entered and stared at the obvious stranger. *What am I doing here? These people will never listen to me. I'm a heathen in their eyes.*

A middle-aged man with short-cropped, receding dark hair and a black kippot on his head strode into the front of the synagogue. He set some papers on a reading table near a dark wooden cabinet that was recessed into the wall on the east side of the worship area. Two scrolls of what appeared to be parchment paper were positioned in the recess in plain view. When the man adjusted his white robe, he revealed a white button-down dress shirt and a powder-blue necktie. After he straightened his tie, his eyes immediately trained on Ben. He smiled and nodded his head once.

Ben squirmed in his seat and shifted his glance away, eager to avoid any direct eye contact with the man Ben assumed was the rabbi. *This was a bad idea. Maybe I should leave now, while I still can.*

The rabbi strode directly back to Ben's row of seats, cornering him. "Shalom, brother. Welcome to our house of prayer. I'm Rabbi Yosef Levitt. Are you visiting the area?"

"Ye-yes," Ben said as he stood and extended his hand. "Ben Chernick." His face slightly reddened. "I'm staying with my daughter and son-in-law here in town."

"I'm glad you joined us. We aren't like some of the synagogues you may have attended in the past. All are truly welcome here. We have no cliques or clusters of elites. I hope you stay after the prayers and reading, for some refreshments. I'm sure our congregants would enjoy meeting you."

The rabbi turned to greet others who were beginning to make their way into the rows of seats. Ben sat down, mildly relieved.

When the prayer service got under way, he vaguely recalled the worship format from his youth. A young man with a long black beard and burgundy-rimmed glasses led a series of songs and prayers that were chanted, followed by the rabbi, who read from the Torah scrolls and delivered a message about honoring God by obeying him.

Thankful when the service ended, Ben turned to leave. A tap on his left shoulder startled and stopped him.

"Bernie Kaplan, here. How are ya? New Yorker, right?"

"Close. I was born in the city, but grew up in Philadelphia."

Ben grasped Kaplan's extended hand and warily eyed the unwanted intruder who had invaded his personal space. *No clean getaway tonight.* Ben judged Kaplan to be in his early seventies. His greased-down white comb-over was partially covered by his kippot. His light green polyester leisure suit and white shoes reminded Ben of a character from an old John Travolta movie. Ben suppressed the urge to smirk.

"You're the first visitor we've had in a while. What brings ya to Palm Coast?" Kaplan asked, his voice unusually loud for the setting.

He stared at Ben with his mouth open, in an aggressive half grin that betrayed his nosiness. His teeth were stained and his skin appeared artificially tanned.

"I'm visiting my daughter and son-in-law. I've stayed to help my son-in-law with his church."

Kaplan took a long look at Ben and stepped back, closing his mouth. "They're not Jewish?" Kaplan's tone was both accusatory and distraught.

"My daughter is, but my son-in-law's a Christian. They both worship at his church. It may be hard to understand, but things happen. I'm a Christian myself now, but I wanted to return to my roots and see if I could be of help."

"So, you're one of those Jews for Jesus, huh? What a sham. You don't even understand your own religion and you want to join a new one! Why don't you stay at your own church, if that's the way you feel?"

Ben felt a surge of strength. He had come to the synagogue to share his personal story about Jesus Christ, and now he would have his say.

"You know, Jesus taught in synagogues at least ten times during his ministry. The synagogue was his place of worship, as it was for the apostle Paul, also a Jew and a former persecutor of Christians. All of Christ's disciples were Jews, and they wrote the New Testament. The practices of my son-in-law's church are based on the synagogue customs Jesus followed. I wanted to come back to the very roots of the Christian faith, but I see I'm not welcome. I'm not surprised, though. I knew this would happen."

"Is that so? And exactly how does a good Jewish boy from Philly get bamboozled into being a heretic?"

"I died and met Jesus. He's real and he wants to know you." Ben was surprised at his own bluntness, while glad he said what he meant.

"Another crazy snowbird." Kaplan's voice was rising. He thrust his palms upward and shook his head. "You're not the first nut job to come here. We don't want your kind around here. Why don't you go back to where you came from?"

By now, several other congregants had gathered around Ben and Kaplan. Rabbi Levitt stood a few feet from the group to listen to the conversation. The group gave a collective groan when Ben mentioned how he met Jesus during his NDE. The rabbi slowly shook his head and turned away.

"Don't worry, I won't come around again and make you uncomfortable. But take it from someone who used to walk in your shoes. Jesus Christ is the true Messiah, whether you like it or not."

Ben stormed out of the synagogue and lurched open his car door. *Bad idea!*

Chapter 5
Climbing Mountains

Dan peered over Walker's shoulder, to the desk in the Major Crimes Investigation building.

"The unusual wounds got my attention," Detective Charlie Walker was saying while he scrolled through a series of grisly crime scene photographs on his large flat screen office monitor. "I thought we were dealing with a typical pedophile homicide, but not after I saw the body. And then the forensic investigator found the circle traced in the soil. I've seen a lot of mutilations, but never one where there were targets drawn on the victim. What does that mean? Why do that to a poor little kid?" asked the detective. He took a swig from a bottle of water.

Dan braced himself on the desk with his left hand and leaned forward to closely examine the horrific close-up color shots of the wounds on the body. *How did Walker handle cases like this and stay sane?* Dan shook his head. "Looks like those target marks might have been put there for others to use, to inflict the wounds. You'd do that if your killers were inexperienced or worse, *forced* to stab the child."

"You mean someone was forced to stab that little girl? How in the world could that happen?"

"Some kind of ritual killing, I'm guessing, but I've heard about cases where others were forced to participate in a murder to avoid being murdered themselves. Others kill for power. Sacrificing the life of another is a way of affirming a contract in the spiritual world. What date was the body discovered?"

"May second. We think the body was dumped overnight. The initial assessment of the coroner for time of death was about eleven at night, May first," Charlie said.

"Sometimes the date of a killing is important. I'll do some checking and see what I can find," Dan promised.

As Walker scrolled through the photos, Dan asked him to stop on the photo of the circle drawn in the sandy Florida soil, around the child's body.

"I've never seen a circle drawn around a homicide victim before, but I don't think it's a coincidence," Dan said. "Someone left you a message. I think the child was killed during some kind of ceremony, and somebody wants you to know about it. Where was the body found?"

"On the grounds of a hunting club. The gate's always left open and the club has acres of woods. Great for hunting *and* for ditching bodies without being seen. We've had quite a few bodies dumped in our county over the years, but none like this one. How did you learn about ritual killings? I didn't think NCIS did those sorts of cases."

"We usually don't. I picked up on it years ago when the supervisory special agent of the Criminal Investigations Squad in our office showed me some photos of the body of a child that had a pentagram in a circle carved in the skin. The case agent had teamed up with some local detectives on the case, and he brought in some books on the occult he was using as references. When he got deeper into the case, he shared bits and pieces with me, but my recollection of the details is hazy because it happened so long ago. I do remember the date of the homicide was significant. I myself never got involved in any ritual killing cases, so I don't have any background info to share with you."

Charlie shook his head and gritted his teeth. "I'm gonna catch the animal who murdered the poor child."

***

The gaunt young man stared in the smudged bathroom mirror, studying his pale skin and sunken eyes. The flashbacks had stopped. He could think for a few minutes. *This must stop. I need help.*

A few strides took him to the middle of the drab living room, where he slumped onto a dingy, dark green corduroy love seat and covered his face with his hands. It was the single piece of furniture in the room, other than a nicked and scratched black wooden table that had a small flat screen TV sitting on it. His mind was clear now, and he remembered why he had moved to the area in the first place. He had told his contacts in the craft that he could be of value to their calling and wanted to join them, but he had a deeper purpose for coming to the state. He stared at his cell phone and tried to muster the courage to call.

After minutes of rehearsing his lines, he gripped the phone and dialed.

On the seventh ring, someone picked up. The hoarse voice of an elderly male answered, "Hello."

The young man froze.

"Hello, hello," the old man repeated.

"Hi, Uncle Peter, this is your nephew. I think my mom told you about me. I wanted to—"

Click. The brief sound of a busy signal filled the young man's ear. He squeezed his eyes shut and fought the tears. Soon he convulsed into sobs and lay, curled tight, on his right side. He knew his uncle was his only hope. He couldn't take the chance of contacting a doctor or a psychologist—they might be members of the craft. Exposure would be a death sentence for him.

After calming himself, he absentmindedly sat up, clicked on the TV, and tuned to a Mickey Mouse cartoon. Clutching a tattered teddy bear, he rocked back and forth on the rigid love seat, pounding the back cushion with his upper body while holding the doll. Soon he became drowsy, the TV droning on with Disney songs in the background. The young man lay down into a partial fetal position and closed his eyes.

***

Dan drained the last few sips of iced tea from his glass and motioned for the female server to come to the table. "I'd like some more tea, please."

As the young woman turned to head back to the kitchen, Dan put down his glass and gazed out of the restaurant's large picture window. He surveyed the south Ponte Vedra beach, where emerald green waves collapsed onto gleaming white sand. Emanations of heat radiated from the smooth, gently sloping beach.

This is why we moved here. Dan felt calmness and relaxation drift over his body while he stared at the beautiful Atlantic Ocean.

Ben put down his grilled grouper sandwich and wiped his mouth with a thick white napkin. "This is a great place. Now I know why you come here. I'd enjoy it better under different circumstances, though."

"What do you mean?"

"I've had a few setbacks lately."

"How so?"

"I have a cardiologist who thinks I'm a mental case, and I nearly got thrown out of a local synagogue. They weren't ready for my testimony, and I wasn't ready to respond like you always are. I don't have the answers to their questions, Dan, and I feel frustrated and inadequate. Tenured professors aren't used to being challenged and belittled. I don't know how I'll ever be able to make the case like you did during our night together in Charlotte."

"What were the questions you couldn't answer?"

"For starters, after I told my cardiologist about my NDEs, he held up a photo of his dead mother who'd been gassed by the Nazis. Told me that if there was a God, she'd still be alive. How do you answer how God could allow people like Hitler to make so many people suffer?"

"You remember, Ben, how we talked about God's covenant with man, to rule the earth like a landlord entrusts his house to a tenant? God sustains the universe and is sovereign over all, but he doesn't control man like a puppeteer. God's not in control of all of man's actions. However, he's definitely in charge of all creation."

Ben perked up and focused on Dan with a steady gaze. He tuned out the din from the crowded restaurant.

Dan continued. "You know God may intervene in the circumstances of our lives, but usually only if we have a relationship with him and ask during prayer. Sometimes his intervention is discipline. And you also know that people commit the evil acts in this world—not God—and their inspiration and motivation either comes from the fallen world around them or internally, from their own sinful nature. In some cases, the motivation comes from the demons who are controlled by Satan. You heard my spiel about the dark kingdom that's temporarily on this earth. It's true, and Hitler was pulled into it. You actually had contact with the dark kingdom during your NDEs. You should be teaching me!"

"But I can't tie it up into neat logical explanations like you can. My experiences defy description. No human can put into words what I saw and felt—though you know I tried. You have the answers at your fingertips, and I just draw a blank."

"That's not true. You remember how we sat in the Charlotte airport terminal all night talking, and how I had to pull out my notes repeatedly to find the scriptural quotes to answer your questions. No one has the Bible completely memorized, except Jesus Christ. Start pinpointing the questions you want to answer and start reading to find the answers." Dan paused a moment.

"But, Ben, I don't know why you're so concerned about being able to answer skeptics—you're an eyewitness! You went to hell three times and were rescued by Jesus! The Savior himself gave you a mission—go tell others about hell! Do you have any idea how rare and precious those moments were, when you were in Christ's presence? You were selected for a mission by God. You have to continue to tell the world about your experience since it's true, and let people decide for themselves. We can't make them listen, but God can. Obey God, that's all."

Ben sat silently and gazed out the window from the quiet corner of the restaurant—a location Dan had obviously selected for privacy. He took in a deep breath and exhaled.

"I'm an academic, Dan. I need quotes and references. No one's going to believe an old Jewish former atheist! I'll be laughed off the lectern!"

"Your NDEs were real—correct?"

"Ah, yes."

"And Christ did tell you to tell others?"

"He did."

"What else do you need?"

"You make it sound so easy, and it's not. … Things have been happening after my heart attacks and NDEs that I haven't told you about. Things I don't understand. Things that, quite frankly, frighten me."

"Like what?" Dan asked while pushing his plate away. He gathered his used napkins and placed them in a pile on top of his plate. He cocked his head to the side and studied Ben's face. He had been around him long enough during their marathon ordeal in the airport to know when Ben was truly rattled.

"I-I … see things," Ben said. "I hear things. I even smell things. Sometimes, when I look at people, I see a dark cloud or a blurry shape hovering over their head. People don't seem to notice or care about them, but I see them. I don't know what they are, but I sense they're bad. Also, I walk by some people and smell sulfur. Other times, when I'm near a person, I smell an exotic, beautiful aroma I've never experienced before. Am I losing my mind?"

"Ben, others who have returned to life after NDEs report seeing entities in the supernatural world. NDEs seem to trigger supernatural gifts in survivors. You most likely saw the physical manifestation of an evil spirit or demon."

"I haven't told you everything," Ben confided. "I've caused light bulbs to burn out prematurely, and I burned out Tim's car radio just by sitting in the passenger seat. It stopped working for no reason!"

"Could be a coincidence."

"Please! You're the one who lectured me that there's no such thing as coincidences, and now you're telling me to ignore strange events that happen right in front of me? I didn't mention this before, but an angel visited me after my last NDE, when Christ rescued me from hell. I was in my hospital room waiting to be taken for some more tests, and a brilliant bluish-white light came into the room. The light formed into a being with a human-like appearance. I knew it was an angel. It came over and touched one of my ankles. I felt a surge of heat pulse through my body, and then it disappeared right before a nurse came in. I was in awe. I felt different, too. I knew all of my medical maladies had been cured—permanently. I just knew. But I can't share my secret angelic encounter with people—they'll think I've lost my mind!"

"See? You're on a mission from God! You have to go out and tell others—you don't have a choice. You can do this. We can do this. You said you don't have the words, but you do! You've experienced a miracle, and you've been commanded to share it with others! I'll go with you and help you answer Biblical questions. I can introduce you to audiences. In a sense I'm an eyewitness, since I was with you all night and the next day and watched you code twice. I told you about the Gospel, and it helped you. You remembered what I kept telling you. Eyewitnesses are the best witnesses, if they're honest and sincere. You're both. Ben, let's go tell the world!"

Ben stared at his amazing friend and exhaled slowly. "All right. I'll do it, and you're coming with me. But first, I've got to take care of a problem."

Chapter 6
Facing Yesterday

Tim pored over piles of church bank statements and invoices. The clutter on the wooden kitchen table appeared to be the result of someone ransacking a filing cabinet. Despite having a part-time finance officer at the church, Tim was sure that if he himself spent enough time with the figures, he could find a way to keep the church's bills paid and the doors open. He had a half-full yellow ceramic mug of lukewarm coffee sitting next to a disheveled pile of bills and deposit slips. He'd been scouring the seemingly endless stack of papers for hours, as if more time would lead to more answers.

His wife Ruth strolled into the kitchen and brought her own brand of sunshine with her. There was something important on her mind, though. He recognized the tiny frown line between her eyes. *What now?*

He forced a grin. "What is it?" he asked, reaching for his coffee mug and preparing to brace himself.

"I got a call from Liz, honey," she said.

"Liz?" *What now? Wasn't losing her husband—my brother— enough?*

The tragic facts flew through Tim's memory: Rob, killed in a freak truck accident the night Dan and Ben were trapped in the Charlotte Douglas International Airport by a massive ice storm. Rob's gasoline tanker truck had skidded on ice and slammed into an electrical substation. The resulting blackouts had triggered Ben's phobia of the dark, three coronaries, and his temporary deaths.

"What did she want, babe?"

"It was about Julie." Ruth stopped, unable to finish her sentence.

Tim stared at her and remained motionless. He could sense bad news coming and, frankly, he was sick and tired of bad news.

"She's been diagnosed with leukemia." Ruth sat on a chair next to Tim and placed a hand on his shoulder.

Tim lowered his head and closed his eyes when he saw the tears in Ruth's. This was crushing news he didn't know if he could handle. Julie was his only niece. An adorable seven-year-old he doted on—particularly since her father was gone. Julie was like a daughter to them—the one they didn't seem able to have. After several minutes with his head bowed, he asked in a shallow, hoarse voice, "Is it curable?"

"Liz said her doctor got the lab results and called them into his office. She said they will fight it, but she sounded broken on the phone." Ruth's voice wavered. She paused.

"It's called juvenile myelomonocytic leukemia. It's a rare type that requires a bone marrow transplant and chemo."

Her flat tone betrayed her inner anguish, but he was unable to offer any comfort. His grief shut him down and left him momentarily speechless.

He watched her pull out a box of brownie mix from the white kitchen cabinet and assemble a metal mixing bowl and clear glass baking dish. She stopped and stared blankly in front of her.

"We'll have to pray," Tim finally said. "I'll contact our prayer team and get the ball rolling. We'll use the best tool we've got—almighty God."

Do I really believe this? What if she's not healed?

***

Ben strolled through the campus quadrangle, toward the faculty office buildings of the historic Pennsylvania academic institution. The university's grounds appeared nearly fully restored and surprisingly neat, considering the campus had been ravaged by a category 4 tornado more than a year earlier. Construction crews were still working on the shell of the new Carson Hall, the university's History Department building, which had been obliterated by the massive funnel cloud.

He felt a sense of comfort and familiarity as he neared the entrance of the 140-year-old serpentine stone building that housed the School of Social Sciences. When he opened the heavy wooden door leading to a stately hallway with high ceilings, the smell of floor polish and stone confronted his nostrils and a moist coolness bathed his face. For many years this had been home for him.

Making the climb to the third floor was surprisingly easy. *I can't believe I'm not out of breath. That angel did heal me!* His emphysema was gone, and his heart felt like it belonged in a sixteen-year-old body. Ben was grinning from ear to ear when he opened the door to his office.

"Dr. Chernick! I didn't know you were coming back to campus. Aren't you still on sabbatical?" Adam, Ben's graduate assistant, asked. He set down a bottle of red fruit drink on the professor's dark wooden desk. Embarrassed at the clutter, he straightened a thick layer of disheveled papers into hasty piles.

Ben was taken aback by being addressed as "Doctor" after many months of being plain old Ben. He hadn't been addressed formally since his brush with death. He preferred the title "Professor," but being called Doctor stoked his badly damaged ego and gave him a surge of pride.

While gathering his thoughts, he slowly scanned the walls of his office which were lined with degrees, certificates, and photos of Ben meeting with academic luminaries who he thought would further his career. The personal shrine to his great academic achievements struck him as shallow and ostentatious. He mentally chided himself for being prideful.

Ben beamed at his assistant. "Had to check on you and make sure everything was functioning smoothly." Ben winked at an incredulous Adam, who was used to seeing a physically frail, mercurial academic who rarely smiled.

Ben said, "I see Professor Schafer is making himself at home. Is he teaching a class now?"

"Yes, he's teaching an intro course and will do a grad course at seven tonight. Are you back for good or just visiting?"

"Oh, I'm only passing through. I had to go by the house to check on a few things before I return to my daughter's home in Florida. My sabbatical ends this fall. I'll be back in time for the next semester. I'm sure Professor Schafer has things under control."

"He does, Professor. Everything's going fine," Adam said.

"I love having an adjunct professor fill in for me. He actually has to work for a living!" Ben surprised himself with his candor. *Why am I suddenly being honest?* Ben felt a disquiet when he realized he had spoken a long-ignored truth in the academic world—tenured professors got higher salaries and ample free time to marinate in their own self-promoting ideas while non-tenured adjunct professors did much of the teaching—or else—for much lower pay.

"Yes, he does, but he hasn't brought much of his own teaching materials with him, other than what you see here," Adam said. "By the way, no one has touched your safe since you left. I've made sure it's still locked and secure—like you wanted."

Ben blushed. He had completely forgotten about the safe and its contents. Pangs of guilt flooded his mind. He'd panicked when the campus had been hit by the tornado the previous April while he was stranded in the Charlotte airport. At the time, he was concerned the safe had been damaged or destroyed. It held what he thought was an important ace in the hole—an incriminating audio recording of his previous mistress who was also his grad assistant at the time. Ben was now deeply ashamed of his cowardly behavior. He felt a strong urge to reach out to the mother of his child and make amends. But would she let him? Did he even deserve her forgiveness?

"I want you to track down a former student of mine," Ben announced. "She worked for me about eighteen years ago." Ben opened the ornate wooden credenza behind his desk, twisted the combination dial on a small gunmetal-gray safe, and pulled out a sealed manila envelope. Slicing it open with a brass letter opener, Ben pulled out a small silver audio recorder and a sheet of paper. After scanning the note, he scrawled out a name on a clean sheet of paper and handed it to Adam.

"A graduate student named Nicole Schmidt had your position years ago, but she left school before graduating. I don't know what happened to her. I want you to try and locate her."

Adam took the piece of paper and, with a quizzical expression, stared at Ben.

Ben was feeling a mixture of relief and intense shame and guilt. He had rebuffed her out of his own selfishness. She'd needed help since her parents had rejected the prospects of a grandchild born out of wedlock, and she had no one else to turn to. Because Ben had been married at the time, he scrupulously hid the affair from his wife and the college faculty. An affair with a student in the late '90s was a career killer and a sure way to end a marriage. Through his cunning and deceit, he had prevented the first, but fell victim to the latter when his arrogance overrode his common sense and prompted him to rebuff his wife rather than seek forgiveness when she learned of his adulterous relationship. Now a lonely divorced man with nothing but his academic career, he felt revulsion over his callous and cruel behavior nearly two decades earlier. He knew deep inside he was the father of Nicole's baby, and he felt a deep-seated need to find the child and make amends.

"Professor.… Professor." Adam broke Ben out of his deep thought. "How soon do you need me to find her?"

"As soon as possible. Once you locate her, let me know right away. Don't contact her, though. I want to handle it personally."

***

Dan Lucas strode into the family room of his Jacksonville, Florida, home and glanced nervously at his watch. *Nine fifty a.m., almost time.*

Connie, his wife, was sitting on the couch checking emails and Facebook posts on her iPad. The house was eerily quiet without the constant chatter and laughter from their three daughters and the grandchildren, now that the kids had all moved away to distant states to start new careers. They sure missed their grandchildren. Still, they were able to stay in touch through the technological miracle of Facetime, which made the separations more bearable.

She was an amazing woman, his wife. She had suffered quietly while he'd cloistered himself in his home office with the door shut, pounding away on his cherished manuscript for months. He wasn't sure if she understood his hibernation was a way of shutting out the distress of Ben's death in the airport the previous year.

Now that he was about to enter a new chapter in his life, in her typical selfless manner she wished him luck in his coming moment of truth.

"You'll do fine, honey. Just be yourself," she said in his direction, where he was pacing back and forth in the kitchen, constantly checking the clock on the stainless-steel stove.

"I know, I know. I hope I'm prepared for his questions," he said while moving back in the direction of their home office, which served as a spare bedroom for guests.

He entered the ten by twelve room lined with bookcases, a filing cabinet, and a large desk with his computer, printer, and office supplies—his inner sanctum.

Dan positioned himself in his office chair and reviewed the notes he had carefully arranged on his desk. He'd been preparing for this moment for weeks. At exactly ten o'clock, he dialed the number which he read from a printed email in front of him.

After four rings, a female voice greeted him. "Lerner and Steele Publishing, may I help you?"

"Yes, this is Dan Lucas. I have a ten o'clock appointment for a teleconference with Mr. Benson. He's expecting my call."

"Yes, Mr. Lucas, I'll connect you."

"Benson." The male voice was flat and authoritative. It carried a wave of strength and certainty.

"Mr. Benson, Dan Lucas here. I have a ten o' clock appointment with—"

"Yes, yes," said Benson, cutting Dan off with a tone of mild impatience.

Wow, this guy's all business. Better get to the point. It doesn't sound like he's into small talk.

"Mr. Benson, you received my proposal and some sample chapters from my manuscript for *From Death to Life*, the nonfiction Christian commentary on near-death experiences."

"Yes." Benson's tone warmed slightly. "My staff reviewed your submission. A thought-provoking subject we might be interested in. You have a good background that would help with marketing. Are you speaking to groups about your former profession, Mr. Lucas? You were in Naval Intelligence?"

"NCIS. Naval Criminal Investigative Service," Dan said, mildly annoyed with the mistake he'd heard countless times before. *Why do people always get the name wrong? Doesn't he watch TV?*

"I've roughed up a few draft presentations, but to be honest, Mr. Benson, I haven't given any talks about NCIS to groups. I wanted people to focus on the message of my book—God is sending people back from clinical death to life again, with a message to share.

God's trying to get people to take the reality of life after death seriously."

"Mr. Lucas, that's all well and good, but scores of books with messages as interesting as yours are published every day. Everyone has a message they want to deliver, particularly Christian writers. Publishing a book like yours is a risk not worth taking unless you're willing to go out in public and connect with potential readers by making yourself interesting. And to do that, you have to talk about what you did for a living. Intelligence is a hot topic right now, and we would need you to share your expertise if we would have any chance of making your book commercially viable. Send us a marketing plan with details about your speaking and social media programs, and we'll get back to you. Good day, Mr. Lucas."

Stunned, Dan had barely said "Thank you" when the connection clicked off.

He'd heard words he didn't want to hear. He wanted to get away from his NCIS career, not resurrect it. He was old news and out of touch with the current NCIS regime. An even greater concern was trying to talk about career experiences that were almost all classified. He didn't want to talk about NCIS; he wanted to deliver a message about God and eternity.

Dan pressed back in his heavily upholstered black leather office chair and stared at the row of books on the wall facing his desk. His mind felt dulled by a sense of crushing defeat and anxiety.

I knew this was going to happen. How did I think I could get away from my past? I hate talking about work. Now they want me to tell stories and sound like a shallow braggart. I'm a failure. ... God, you'll have to use me in another way.

Chapter 7
Getting Clarity

Pastor Tim Williams shifted his lanky six-foot-two-inch frame uncomfortably on the brown metal folding chair at the back of the partially lit Radiant Love Church fellowship hall. He remained quiet while he watched a group of teenagers at the far end of the room.

Between glances at their phones, the group of a half dozen engaged in lighthearted banter—oblivious to their pastor's stealthy entrance. He was partially obscured from view by a stack of folding chairs on a wheeled metal storage rack. Tim had deliberately arrived late to be present when the group dispersed for the night. Their group leader, Garen, had already left for the evening after presenting a talk on maintaining Christian values in a secular world, and most of the youth had remained to finish their drinks and socialize around several tables.

Tim was proud of his church's youth ministry, and rightly so. He and Ruth had built it from the ground up—starting with one student. They poured their hearts and souls into the program. However, as the preteens had matured into high school and college students, a sizable percentage had stopped attending. Tim was at a loss to explain why, since some of them went to a local college.

Dressed in black jeans and a purple-and-white-checkered button-down shirt, Tim had positioned himself to say good-bye to the group while they went by him to leave the building at the hall's rear exit. His goal was to pull one of the youths aside and casually elicit information about some of the missing students.

"Oh, hi, Pastor. I didn't see you come in. Good night," said one of the students as he passed Tim, who had stood up next to the stack of chairs.

"Good night," Tim answered with a warm voice. "See you next week!"

One by one, the students left.

"Jeremey," Tim called out to a slight youth with black-rimmed glasses and an olive complexion who was strolling by. The startled teen, not expecting to see the pastor, stopped in front of Tim.

He was an eighteen-year-old college freshman who'd grown up in the church. His family had moved to Radiant Love within several months after the doors had opened, and his parents were welcoming and supportive of Tim and Ruth.

The families had socialized and become close over the past several years. Tim felt comfortable talking informally with Jeremey; he knew Jeremey's parents trusted him and would have no problem with the impromptu chat.

"Hey, Jeremey. I haven't seen Tom or Sandra or Beth in quite a while. Did they move away or start going to another church?"

"No, Pastor Tim, they're still around. They must be busy with schoolwork." Jeremey glanced away in an awkward attempt to avoid eye contact.

"You seem to have enough time to stay with the youth group. Is school really so tough this year?"

The young man seemed to struggle to find the right words. "I've, um, tried to get them to come back, Pastor Tim, but they say they're bored with church. They say they don't fit in anymore."

"Why do you think they've changed their attitudes toward church?"

"I think they're trying to figure out how they fit into the world. They hear one thing in church and then they hear the opposite everywhere else. They're not sure church is relevant anymore."

Tim paused for a minute to process Jeremey's information. He couldn't honestly claim he understood his young friend. "Can you give me some specifics? Help me to understand what I'm missing?"

"Pastor Tim, they're tired of being told to be a good person, to have strong faith, and to love other people like Jesus did. They already know that. They know the stories about the disciples and the birth, death, and Resurrection of Jesus Christ. They want something new. They know the morals of the world are going downhill. They're not interested in the Bible's stories. They want something more, and for them, college gives them what they're searching for."

Tim was surprised. He felt if he used the Bible as the bedrock for all the church's teachings, he'd be on solid ground and able to reach people of all ages. The truth was the truth, after all; it was God's word. Of course, there was a lot of repetition in Tim's sermons, but people needed to hear the complete story of Christ's life and all those who were part of his world to become faithful followers of Christ—or so he had thought.

"So, you're saying they're not being intellectually challenged?"

"Pastor Tim, they don't see any evidence in the world of God's existence, and they don't see any reason to believe an old book—sorry, their words—full of stories written by old men thousands of years ago. They don't feel like they're rejecting God because they don't think he's made himself known to them in any real way. A lot of our professors tell us man and the universe are an accident. I don't believe them, but after you keep hearing it over and over again from so many different teachers, it starts to have an effect on you. My friends don't feel like they're rejecting God. They feel that's the way God made them—to be on their own. They don't feel a connection to God. They feel a connection to this life and this world."

Tim tried to read Jeremey's face—probing for signs that might help him to respond in a compassionate and reasoned way. How could he reach these young people if it wasn't through the Bible? If the truth didn't work, what else could he do? He slowly shook his head, feeling more like he'd been kicked in the gut by a mule than enlightened by one of his young members.

Jeremey sighed, his thin shoulders slumping a bit. "Sorry, Pastor Tim. I know it's not what you want to hear, but it's the truth."

***

Detective Charlie Walker was startled by the loud ringtone of his cell phone as he read a draft investigative report forwarded by one of his investigators. He clicked the mouse to close the document on his screen.

"Walker."

"Detective Walker, this is Joe Pearson with the Tampa PD's Major Crimes Bureau. Thanks for contacting us. I think you may have the body of one of our missing children in your morgue."

"Sorry to hear that—but glad you might have resolved a case," Walker said.

"I'm sending Detective Susan Noals over to identify the body. We were starting to think this child abduction case was going to remain unresolved, until we got your bulletin and saw the National and Florida Crime Information Center entries. I hope the body of the little girl you have isn't our missing child, but based on the description and the morgue photos, I'd say it's very possible. We're going to withhold notification of the family until we confirm the identity of the child's remains."

Walker inhaled deeply and leaned forward. He glanced at a large gold picture frame on his desk with a color photo of his wife and three children. His mind briefly flashed the image of the dead child's body lying in the woods. He shuddered while he mentally pictured the mournful expression on the little girl's face. He snapped his attention back to the phone call.

"I need to thank you, Detective Pearson. Your squad is on the ball. Picking up on our crime bulletin as quickly as you did will save us all a lot of time and hopefully lead to a resolution of both of our cases."

"Appreciate that. We got lucky with this one too, considering we never got a single response to our amber alert. We do have good dental records, though … and some DNA samples from the child's hair ties. We should be able to confirm or rule out the identity one way or another."

Walker's grief and anguish slowly melted away as the conversation continued, and he decided to press into the details of the case.

"Joe, I know your detective will bring the case file with her when she comes to view the body, but could you give me a synopsis of the case? We've run out of leads on this one."

"Sure. The victim's family reported the child was playing by herself in the backyard sandbox, as she always did in the late morning. The yard was enclosed by a wooden privacy fence with a rear gate that was closed but not locked. The mother did regular visual checks of the child through a glass slider, and when she went into the laundry room to get a load of clothes out of the dryer, she heard a muffled scream, the gate banging, and a car driving off. The abduction took place in less than thirty seconds.

"When she got to the back door and ran outside, she could hear a car speeding away. The gate was open and still swinging back and forth. The privacy fence blocked her view of the vehicle and she never saw any of the subjects. We didn't find any trace evidence at the scene, and there weren't any security cameras nearby. We don't have any witnesses in the neighborhood, either. It was a planned abduction. They knew where the child would be that morning. So far, we haven't developed any leads—at least not until you posted your bulletins. Now we have the body two hundred miles away. I know that no two abduction cases are the same, but this one surprises me."

Walker felt a mixture of relief and apprehension. *Why would anyone transport a child's body so far away to dump it? They greatly increased their chances of getting caught.*

Walker caught himself having a one-way mental conversation and refocused on his phone call. "We were beginning to think we were never going to solve this case when no one came forward to report a missing child in our area. We couldn't figure out how a child could go missing without someone noticing. Now we know how."

***

Dan Lucas gently eased his metallic-blue Dodge Charger into the Williams' driveway and lightly tapped the horn twice. The deep rumble of the massive Hemi V8's idling cut through the cool morning air.

The quiet suburban Palm Coast community seemed deserted. Not another person or vehicle stirred in the early morning hour. The now-familiar trim outline of Ben Chernick appeared in the doorway of the cream-colored stucco home. He marched briskly toward the waiting car. Dan felt a calming bond of friendship while he watched the supernaturally remodeled version of Ben Chernick enter the passenger side of the car. Ben's salt-and-pepper hair was starting to show a lot more salt than pepper.

"Wow, this is some ride! I didn't know you were into fast cars," Ben said.

"There's a lot of things you don't know about me," Dan said with a chuckle. "This is my midlife crisis car. I'm sure you have your toys too."

"I did. I indulged in fine wines and antique furniture for most of my adult life. Seems like a lot of wasted money now. Since my NDEs, I've lost interest in material things. You, of all people, should understand."

Ben paused as he inspected the interior of Dan's high-performance car and ran his hands over the light brown leather seats.

"This is an impressive machine. Shows great care, too. Does it have an ashtray?"

Dan laughed. "I thought you quit smoking. After all you've been through, you're still thinking about cigarettes?"

"Oh, I don't smoke anymore, but riding in a car always reminds me of my smoking days. I had a soda can in my car that was always full of ashes. I chain-smoked almost a quarter of a pack every day during my commute to and from campus."

"Ben, most cars haven't had ashtrays in years. Glad to hear you stopped smoking, though. I remember those coughing fits you had in the Charlotte airport. A couple of times, I thought you were a goner. Good thing you kept your inhaler with you then. … By the way, how's your emphysema?"

"It's gone. I guess when God gave me a new heart, he threw in a new set of lungs too. You know, I've even forgotten about all the wheezing and shortness of breath attacks you saw me have in Charlotte. Ruth is very proud of me too—she hated my smoking." Ben realized he was bragging, and he blushed slightly and turned toward the window. He glanced back at Dan. "Now, where, again, are you taking me, my friend?"

"I needed to take a ride and clear my head about work. I haven't seen you since your trip to Philly, so I thought this would be a good time for us to talk, during the drive. Besides, you always seem to inspire me."

"Are you back working again? I thought retirement was the big prize you'd always been waiting for."

"Oh, I'm still technically retired, but I have to treat my book writing like a job, or I get pulled away by a lot of distractions. I need to do some brainstorming about where I'm headed with my writing. That's why I asked you to come along for a ride and get some coffee. I wanted to talk with you—face-to-face. Like we did in Charlotte for all those hours in the terminal. We were honest with each other—often blunt. I need your feedback, Ben. I need to figure out what to do next and I want your advice."

"My advice?" Ben laughed. "If I recall correctly, you were the guy with all the answers, and all I could do was take cheap shots at your very sound ideas. You crushed me in our little all-night debate. I never thought I'd be able to admit that, Dan, but it's true."

"I suspect God was in the midst of our conversation. But now I need some more of your candor. You've never been shy about telling me how you feel about a subject." Dan paused for a second and narrowed his eyes while maintaining his attention on the road ahead.

"Last Thursday I had a talk with a publisher who's interested in my book. The only problem is, as a condition for giving me a contract, he wants me to get out on the speaking circuit and start talking about my old job, to help sell the books. He says I don't have a chance unless I sell myself and my former profession with NCIS. That's exactly what I don't want to do. I want my book to focus people on God and the veracity of the Bible, not my little world of chasing bad guys and catching spies."

Ben's expression was pure astonishment. "I can't believe I'm hearing you say this. You were the guy who spent an entire night talking about your old career and tying it to facts that prove God exists. I heard nothing but asset validation, lie detectors, and interrogation techniques to get to the truth, and now you're telling me you don't want to talk about it!"

"But that was different. We were having a private discussion. I wasn't making a public presentation."

"It could have been, and maybe it should be," Ben said. "I still think about some of those cases you told me about. They were fascinating! Remember when someone reported some inside information about Islamic terrorists who were going to drive a truck bomb into a US consulate overseas? You ran a major operation and determined the inside source made it all up. You never told me where it took place, but you had such a detailed recollection that I knew it was real. It was a great example of how a fabricator can muck up your work and a good tie-in to your point about how people seeking facts about God have to always be on the alert for false messengers."

"Yeah, that was a real case, but it was just an example I used for the sake of making a point."

"Exactly. And it worked perfectly. And how about the spy case you laid out so eloquently, involving the US Marine Corps officer? I was on the edge of my seat, but I didn't want you to know I was listening to every word. You were convinced he was working for a foreign spy, but when you brought him in for interrogation, you determined you had the wrong man. I didn't say anything at the time, but I was very impressed with your integrity. I knew then the evidence you cited to prove God exists was based on unbiased facts you had gathered—honestly—without filtering them through your own biases. I knew then, Dan, the truth meant more to you than scoring a point in a debate. It was your character that carried your message. Your publisher is right. You need people to see the real Dan Lucas, and when they do, they'll be open to your message and interested in your book."

Dan gripped the leather-wrapped steering wheel tightly and stared straight ahead. *Is my own ego getting in the way of what God wants me to do? Is it about his will or mine?* After collecting his thoughts, he turned his head and briefly stared at Ben before shifting his eyes back to the road.

"All right, you convinced me. I need to get out and tell war stories. But you're coming with me."

As Dan's words trailed off inside the car's interior, the melodic ringtone of Ben's phone partially masked the throaty rumble of the car's engine. Ben took the call.

"Hello... You did? You work fast!" Ben turned his head toward the passenger window and said, "Send me an email with all the info, and lock up any papers you have that contain the details. I'll take it from here. Good work!"

Ben ended the call and remained silent. Dan turned and saw that Ben was deep in thought.

"Everything all right?"

"That was Adam, my grad assistant. He's located my former mistress and the mother of my child."

***

A smartly dressed and fit middle-aged man stopped his black Range Rover with the prized black alloy rims and sat quietly while he scanned the neighborhood for signs of movement. He studied the drab two-story dwelling and scrutinized it for entrances. He looked up and down the street for a particular vehicle, but saw none. The driveway of the house was empty.

He glanced down at his phone to reread the text message containing the address. *Yep, this is the right place.* He carefully got out of the car and closed the door slowly to avoid making noise. He carried a black leather bag in his left hand as he strode quietly toward the home, all the while watching for others who might have witnessed his arrival. The tranquil street with an old Florida atmosphere was eerily silent. An occasional dog bark and the chirp of a bird punctuated the humid First Coast sunset. The sandy soil of the front yard clung to his black leather Florsheims. He loosened the collar of his light-yellow Brooks Brothers dress shirt while scanning the area to ensure no one was watching his advance.

He climbed steps to a second-story entrance and knocked on the door.

"Hello, hello. Little brother, are you there? I'm Dr. Garvin. You don't know me, but your family sent me to check on you." He stopped to listen for sounds of activity inside. He continued to address the mold-streaked brown metal door with a singsong voice that was punctuated by rhythmic pauses.

"They're worried about you. … Your family misses you. … They love you. … Your family needs you. … You're so special to them. … Why are you so distant? … They really want to hear from you."

No answer.

The man opened his black bag and pulled out a small stainless-steel instrument that resembled a dental tool. He inserted it into the front door lock. Within thirty seconds, a soft click pierced the muggy air that hung on the man's shoulders like a damp shower curtain. He turned the corroded metal knob and stepped into the darkened apartment. The still air in the room was warm, humid, musty.

"Hello, hello."

No answer.

The man turned on an overhead light and carefully searched through the dingy apartment to confirm it was empty. He returned to the living room and placed a black metal ring behind a cushion on the tattered love seat.

"Here's a present. It will bring some very nice visitors to keep you company."

He turned off the light. After slowly closing the front door of the apartment, he headed down the mold-stained wooden steps that creaked under his weight.

You got away this time, but I'll be back. You won't be so lucky next time.

Chapter 8
Past Is Prologue

Ben relished his time alone when he could concentrate on his Bible-in-a-Year reading plan. So much to learn! He took a sip of his almond milk, banana, and kale smoothie and set the tall glass next to his laptop on a small wooden desk.

The soft glow of the laptop's screen illuminated the desk as he scrolled through a passage of Scripture in his digital Bible. This early morning, the soft whoosh of the computer fan was the only sound in an otherwise quiet house.

The readings often triggered flashbacks of his NDEs and his time in the presence of Christ. Somehow, the vivid memories helped him interpret Scripture on a deeper level. He clicked the Bible study app closed and leaned back in the tan desk chair. Clasping the back of his neck with his hands, he stared blankly into the softly lit room. He had so much to be thankful for.

Feeling warm from an earlier two-mile trek through the neighborhood, he stirred from his mental escape and unzipped his summer-weight maroon-and-white workout jacket. He adjusted the height of the chair. Ben had become increasingly comfortable in his home away from home—a small spare bedroom where he had taken up temporary residence after his daughter, Ruth, had flown him to Palm Coast from Charlotte, North Carolina, to recuperate.

She had brought Ben into her home after his short-lived clinical death in a Charlotte hospital following his third heart attack, after they hadn't spoken for nearly sixteen years.

Ben had created the falling-out when he had refused to attend her wedding. He had judged Tim an unworthy husband for his daughter because he lacked a college education and wasn't Jewish. But after Ben's brush with death, he had humbled himself and begged Ruth for forgiveness. As a result of those events and life lessons, Ben felt he'd been blessed with a real family. He savored his time with his daughter and son-in-law.

Returning his attention to the computer, Ben scrolled through his email inbox and clicked on an email from Adam, his graduate assistant. *Am I ready for more truth? More reckonings?* He furrowed his brow as he gazed at the screen and read the message.

"Dear Professor Chernick, like I told you on the phone, I located your former grad assistant, Nicole Schmidt. It wasn't hard to find her. She's become very successful. You must have been a great mentor for her. She's now an assistant professor of sociology at Temple University in Philadelphia."

Ben wiped his face with a handkerchief while he stared at the screen in disbelief. *Wow, assistant professor at Temple! I'm impressed!* Ben's pulse quickened.

"I followed your instructions and didn't contact her to verify any of the information I developed, so I'm not sure if it's all current. She lives in a condo on North Eighth Street, and her office is in Glatfelter Hall, located at 1115 Polett Walk, Philadelphia.

"I couldn't find any references to a husband or any children, so I assume she has never married. Anyway, I hope this is what you wanted. If you need more details, let me know. Take care, Professor, and enjoy your sabbatical! Adam."

Ben swallowed hard and read the last paragraph several times. Tears came to his eyes and he closed them tight. *She didn't keep the baby!* He rested his head on his folded arms. The weight of his guilt and remorse was crushing. *Why, God, why?*

His plea rang hollow. He knew the answer.

***

When Tim pulled into the parking lot of the Radiant Love Church, he saw Dan's gleaming car already there. The church was Tim's passion—a passion he'd always been sure was God's will for him. Now, losing sleep over the bills, the tenuous faith of his young adult members, his niece's declining health, and the mental health of his father-in-law, Tim wondered if God hadn't left him to wander in his own desert. He wasn't even sure if he was ready to hear what Dan had to say today, but he was unable to postpone their meeting again.

Lord, help me listen with your heart and your wisdom. I'm coming to understand how insufficient my own is.

He pushed open the car door and grabbed the carrier with the steaming cups of coffee. *Okay, here we go.*

The aroma of full-bodied coffee wafted through the small slits of the white plastic cup covers and drifted into the still air of the church's conference room, where Dan was busy sorting through a briefcase. Tim placed the tray on the conference room table and extended a hand to Dan.

"You're early," Dan said with a warm tone.

"Yeah, couldn't sleep, so I got up before the alarm went off. A lot on my mind lately. Been thinking about the church and all." Tim paused while he surveyed the conference room and pressed his lips. "Brought us something to keep us awake. You retired agents like to start early, don't you?"

Dan glanced at his watch. "Heck, this is midday for me," he said with a raised brow. "Needed this coffee, though. Thanks."

He arranged an English Standard Version Bible in a plain brown leather cover, a spiral notebook, and a stack of blue paper folders on the table.

"Okay, let's get down to business," Dan announced as he snapped the lock closed on his briefcase and placed it on the floor. He quickly sifted through the stack of folders, pulled out one, and opened it. He read silently while his finger traced some typewritten notes on a sheet of paper. After about a minute, with a broad grin he looked up at Tim.

"You told me some of your congregation, particularly some of the younger ones, couldn't accept the concept of a loving God who would order his followers to slaughter complete villages of men, women, and children, and animals."

"It sure is hard to understand," Tim said. "I don't doubt God is all-loving, but I don't have any answers for them. I tell them we must have faith and trust God, even if we don't understand what he does. Lean not on your own understanding, I tell them. I know that's a weak answer, but it's all I can come up with."

"How can they love a God if they think he indiscriminately slaughters innocent people?" Dan asked. "How could anyone love a God who kills women and children and their animals for no reason? I couldn't. No one could."

"Exactly my point. I don't even understand," Tim stated.

"All right, since we know God is loving yet also just and holy, there must be an answer." Dan closed the blue folder.

"What if I told you God was destroying people and animals with genetic mutations? Mutations that were deliberately caused by supernatural beings created by God, who left their assigned stations of governance in the heavenly realm, who came to earth in physical form, who impregnated human women, and created a genetic bloodline of gigantic half-human, half-angels who lacked a human soul that could be redeemed by God. Beings that had no hope of salvation—no hope of spending eternity with God and Jesus Christ because they weren't made in God's image. What if I also told you the animals that were destroyed were hybrids caused by genetic manipulation?"

Tim swallowed hard and peered at Dan while thinking, *This guy's as crazy as Ruth's dad is.*

"I know you're a smart guy with lots of experience," Tim said. "I know you wrote a book, and my father-in-law respects you. But with all due respect, where in the Bible is there proof for any of this?"

Dan nodded slowly, glanced at the table, and reestablished eye contact with Tim. "I expected that question and I understand. You're relying on what you were taught in seminary and on what your fellow pastors believe. You weren't exposed to a full examination of the Scriptures because of the church's tendency to spiritualize any of the content of the Bible that describes the supernatural. I suspect your professors glossed over it."

"I'm not sure what you mean. We studied all of the Bible in seminary."

"Not really, or we wouldn't be having this discussion. Where do I start?" Dan pulled out his Bible and opened it to a bookmarked page.

"I guess the best place is in the Bible where the subject is first introduced." Dan traced a line on a page in his Bible. "Here, Genesis 6, verses 1 and 2. 'When man began to multiply on the face of the land and daughters were born to them, the sons of God saw that the daughters of man were attractive. And they took as their wives any they chose. Verse 4. The Nephilim were on the earth in those days and also afterward when the sons of God came into the daughters of men and they bore children to them. These were the mighty men of old, the men of renown.' " Dan looked at Tim and waited for a response.

"Okay," Tim stated. "What about it? Those passages refer to warriors taking brides—the spoils of war, I suppose. You know, the survival of the fittest, and in this case the conquerors took women when they wanted them. The Bible is full of stories like that. I'm not sure what your point is."

"Tim, you're not comprehending the words as they're written. You're translating them through a modern prism of twenty-first-century Christian thought, with no appreciation for the interaction between man and supernatural beings before and during Noah's time. Notice the passage makes a distinction between the sons of God and the daughters of man. Who do you think the sons of God were?"

"I don't know. In a way, we're all sons of God, at least through our relationship with Jesus Christ."

"There's a reason the Bible is written that way. Throughout the Scriptures, the literal translation of the Hebrew words for sons of God is angels or angelic beings. You can do the research yourself. And then, to erase any doubt about what the passages are talking about, the term *Nephilim* is used. Do you know what they are?"

"I don't. Some kind of warrior or nobility?"

"No, Nephilim are giant half-humans with partial supernatural ancestry—the fallen angels. Giants and fallen angels are mentioned in more than twenty verses in the Bible. The majority of ancient biblical versions, including the Septuagint, Theodotion, Latin Vulgate, Samaritan Targum, Targum Onkelos, and the Targum Neofiti, interpret the word Nephilim to mean 'giants.' Other ancient scholars translate it to mean 'fallen ones.' Doesn't that make you curious? Why would there be a race of giants in the early days, and why are they called fallen? Every human being on earth is tainted by a sinful nature and is fallen in God's eyes. Isn't it interesting that the Nephilim are specifically singled out in the Bible as fallen? Fallen from where?"

Tim remained silent. *Can any of this be true? Is this an accurate interpretation? How could I have missed every single reference to these beings?*

To relieve any pressure on Tim, Dan answered the questions the next moment. "I'd say the evidence points to a fall from the heavenly realm. And what was the result of the commingling of angelic and human DNA besides enormous size? Some of the Bible verses describe the giants as having particular physical characteristics, including having six fingers and six toes on each hand and foot. They were also extremely aggressive and prone to cannibalism, in addition to being large enough to kill an average human with their bare hands. And when I say giant, I don't mean abnormally tall with a normal frame, like we have today when folks grow over seven feet tall. I also don't mean people who suffered from the abnormality of gigantism. I mean real giants with massive bodies of enormous girth and strength. Eight, ten, twelve, fifteen feet, and sometimes much larger."

Dan pulled out another folder and scanned a page with his right index figure. He paused for a moment and shifted his gaze toward the bank of windows lining the meeting room's outer wall before speaking.

"Here, Amos 2:9, 'Yet I destroyed the Amorites before them, though they were tall as the cedars and strong as the oaks. I destroyed their fruit above and their roots below.' Here's another one, Numbers 13:33, 'We saw the Nephilim there'—the descendants of Anak come from the Nephilim. 'We seemed like grasshoppers in our own eyes, and we looked the same to them.' Almost every translation of the Bible refers to them as Nephilim and as giants. Many other verses refer to giants as well. Most everyone knows the story of David and Goliath. But do you realize Goliath came from a family of giants?"

"Not really, but why is any of this important? So what, if there were giants in biblical times. What does that have to do with God ordering the slaughter of men, women, and children?"

"What do we do with people infected with a highly contagious, incurable, deadly disease?"

"We quarantine them, I suppose."

"And what if they try to escape and mix with the population?"

"We do everything in our power to stop them."

"Would you use force if necessary?"

"I guess so."

"God was forced to do exactly the same thing. Once the fallen half-angel, half-human babies matured, they began mating and having children of their own and passing on their soulless mutant genes—in some respects, creating a new generation of what we would think of today as giant zombies. If God allowed them to continue to multiply, they would have eventually taken over the world, and God would've been left without a single human being who could be saved to spend eternity with him. More importantly, it would have prevented the birth of Jesus Christ. Satan planned to pollute the world with evil mutants, and God had to stop it. I strongly believe all of those villages God ordered destroyed had genetic mutants. That's why even women and children had to be destroyed. And that's why God caused the worldwide flood. The Nephilim were poised to take over the world, and God had to stop it. That's why he chose Noah and his genetically pure family to be saved in the ark. After the flood, the Nephilim reappeared, and God was forced to order their slaughter again."

"Dan, why aren't other people talking about this? Those Scriptures you quoted sound like they're talking about giants, but you're taking them out of context. If this was so important, they would have covered it in seminary and we'd be addressing it in sermons."

"You bring up an important point. It's a real problem in the churches today, which explains why we don't talk about it. Sometime in the past, the church was getting pushback for the supernatural content of the Bible and, later, some of the amplifying ancient extra-biblical texts like the Book of Enoch. This was the time when man was supposedly becoming rational and learning about science.

"To make the Bible relevant and in sync with the emerging culture, there was a move to deemphasize the supernatural aspects of the Bible and spiritualize a lot of its content to make it palatable to those of the new culture and the Age of Enlightenment. Then the theory of evolution was introduced into the culture, and the presence of giants thousands of years ago didn't fit into the Darwinian narrative, so all evidence of it had to be ignored and often destroyed."

"Evidence? What evidence? I don't remember ever hearing about it anywhere."

"I'm talking about books and, more recently, newspapers. There's an established record of many newspaper articles about huge skeletons being found in America and other countries. You can check the microfiche records yourself. Here, let me give you a couple of examples."

Dan eyed his stack of blue folders and pulled out one from the middle. After opening it, he removed a sheet of paper and read the contents silently.

Within a few moments, he said, "Right. Here's one of many hundreds of examples. This is an article from the *Fitchburg Sentinel*, written on January 16, 1904. Fitchburg is in Massachusetts. The title of the article is 'A Gigantic Skeleton—Bones of a man eleven feet in height.' The article goes on to say, 'Winnemucca, Nevada, Jan. 16.—Workmen engaged in digging gravel here have uncovered a number of bones that were once part of the skeleton of a gigantic human being. Dr. Camels pronounced them bones of a man who must have been eleven feet in height.' This article came from the newspaper's archives."

Dan paused and continued to scan the paper. "Here's another one. *New York Times*, March 17, 1924. The headline is 'Find Skeleton of Giant. Idaho Road Men Dig Up Bones of Prehistoric Herbivorous Woman.' The article begins with, 'Lewiston, Idaho, March 16. Associated Press. A huge skeleton, believed to be that of a prehistoric human being, has been discovered in the Salmon River country, south of here, by two members of the State Highway Department who have brought their find to the city. The lower jaw and vertebrae will be sent to the Smithsonian Institution at Washington, DC, for analysis as to the probable date of existence. The bones were found in the side of a cliff at a depth estimated to be fifty feet. Nearly the entire skeleton was discovered. Measuring more than eight feet in height and possessing numerous strange features, the skeleton has aroused widespread interest. Three physicians pronounced it to be that of a woman.' "

Dan handed Tim a copy of the articles as he continued to speak. He reached into the folder and pulled out another sheet of paper. He scanned the page and resumed commenting.

"Here's another one. '*New York Tribune*—February 3, 1909. Skeleton 15 feet tall unearthed in Mexico.' The article goes on to say, 'News was recovered here Monday from Mexico that at Ixtapalapa, a town 10 miles southeast of Mexico City, there had been discovered what was believed to be the skeleton of a prehistoric giant of extraordinary size. A peon, while excavating for the foundation of a house on the estate of Augustine Juarez, found the skeleton of a human being that is estimated to have been about 15 feet tall.' So, Tim, you can see there is more than a mere smattering of evidence of these gigantic beings."

Tim sat motionless, with the papers in his hand. *Is this for real?*

"Even Abraham Lincoln referred to giants in an article he wrote in 1848, about the magnificence of Niagara Falls." Dan pulled out another sheet of paper.

"Here it is, the quote from Lincoln. 'The eyes of that species of extinct giants, whose bones fill the mounds of America, have gazed on Niagara, as ours do now.' The mounds he's probably referring to are located in the Ohio Valley and in other states. Scores of newspaper articles from the late 1800s to the mid-1900s document the discovery of giant bones and skeletons in burial mounds in the United States and other countries. The Italian island of Sardinia is loaded with the bones of giants, but any time a local finds them during excavation, government officials arrive and confiscate the bones. Some say the giant skeletons are often discovered with gold and silver jewelry and other artifacts and that's why they're seized. But if that's true, why don't the authorities put the precious relics in a museum and let the locals see the skeletons, as they do with dinosaur bones?"

When Tim was about to answer, Dan cut him off.

"You know, the accounts of the discovery of giant skeletons aren't just documented in American newspapers." Dan pulled out another sheet of paper and quickly skimmed it. "For example, Reginaldo de Lizarraga, a Dominican friar, wrote a book in the late 1500s about his explorations in South America and the discovery of graves of giants in Córdoba, Argentina."

Tim put down the copy of the newspaper article and stared at Dan. "If these newspaper reports are true—and I assume they are—why wouldn't the bones be on display in museums? And more importantly, how could these discoveries be covered up?"

Dan laced his fingers behind his head and grinned in Tim's direction. "Let me answer your second question first. When many of these giant skeletons were discovered in the 1800s and 1900s, we didn't have the personal communication capabilities we have today. Think about it. We didn't start to have personal computers until about thirty years ago, and the World Wide Web for the internet wasn't developed until about the same time. As you know, in the old days, people didn't have the technical capabilities to instantly photograph an object and send it to their friends and colleagues or do video recordings. Reports had to be done longhand or on a typewriter and sent by telegraph or mail. Heck, the modern telephone wasn't widely available until around the mid-1900s. People couldn't record and share information like we can today."

Tim slumped in a chair and held his head in the palms of his hands. If he taught any of this stuff in his sermons, he'd have no congregation at all. And he and Ruth would be the laughingstock of North America. *Would the young people be interested in these tales and theories, tales they never heard of before?*

Dan continued speaking. "As far as the cover-up is concerned, when I began my study of the large body of evidence that pointed to the past existence of giants on the earth, I also discovered a concerted effort to make sure the giant skeletons never made it into museums or on display. To start with, most of the finds were made during farming, construction, or commercial excavations. Unless a technical expert took control of the discovery site, the easiest course of action would be to throw the bones away or rebury them.

"Farmers and excavation workers didn't have the time or training to be archaeologists. But in those newspaper reports that document the bones were to be turned over to the Smithsonian or other museums, you have to stop and focus on the museums to get an idea of what motivated them to take certain actions."

Dan took a sip of his coffee. "First, the Smithsonian is funded almost entirely by the federal government. Second, the Smithsonian's National Museum of Natural History is an altar to the wonders of evolution. To my knowledge, the Smithsonian exhibits don't mention even the possibility of an intelligent designer, much less a divine Creator. God is completely excluded from the story of man's appearance on earth. The acknowledgment of the existence of a giant race of humans would clash with the evolutionary narrative of man evolving from a single-celled organism over the millennia to the advanced species that we are today. Plus, the acknowledgment of the existence of ancient giants would destroy the narrative that Native Americans were the first and only inhabitants of North America before the arrival of the early colonists. Historians and academics would have to acknowledge that our current understanding of history is wrong." Dan reached for his coffee.

"All right," Tim said, "I understand how the discoveries could have been covered up before modern communication technologies became available, but if someone finds a giant skeleton today, they have a way of getting the word out fast. So, how come people aren't talking about this today on college campuses and in the media? Why aren't archeologists and paleoanthropologists out in the fields looking for more finds? Surely, there must be more skeletons out there that can be discovered. At least a bone or something should still be around."

"Oh, there is fieldwork being done by a select group of Bible scholars and researchers, but their findings aren't covered by any mainstream media outlets or academic organizations that I'm aware of. Just the opposite. There is a dedicated effort, in my view, to discredit and delegitimize them. Worse, those same efforts are attempting to minimize and trivialize the whole subject of giant human skeletons so that it's treated with the same disdain as the topic of Bigfoot."

"Dan, I'm surprised to hear you say that. I never thought you'd be into conspiracy theories."

"Oh, I'm not, but I have thirty years of experience running counterintelligence and counterespionage operations, and I know how governments spend a lot of time and money trying to deceive each other about new weapons systems and war plans through deception operations. I can spot the deception methodology a mile away. For example, if you google *Smithsonian destruction of giant human skeletons*, you'll get a website called worldnewsdailyreports.com, which purports to discuss the topic in detail. In reality, it's a bogus site that runs deception articles, and if you scroll to the very bottom of the site, you'll find a disclaimer that states the website is satirical in nature and the content is fictional. The bottom of the website lists New World Order Media as the purveyor. In my view, they want to take a serious topic, appear to make a legitimate effort to explore it by presenting some real facts, but in reality they want to trivialize it so serious researchers and the curious will stay away."

Dan glanced down and studied a piece of paper. "Another website, listverse.com, has an article titled '10 Forbidden and Creepy Claims of Giant Human Skeletons.' It also has a link to the bogus report from the worldnewsdailyreport site, which instantly discredits the entire article, even though most of it is accurate and truthful. It's an operational technique that conditions people to consider all such articles as false and therefore not worthy of their interest. The title, '10 Forbidden and Creepy Claims of Giant Human Skeletons' is also a blatant attempt to stigmatize the entire topic. Have you ever seen archeology or paleoanthropology described as 'creepy' or 'forbidden' fields of study? In this day and age, when the simple click of a mouse takes you out of an article, the use of inflammatory words will repel most serious-minded people and keep it on the fringes of conspiracy theories. That's one reason it's not discussed and studied in wider circles."

Tim remained silent. He could feel his own anxiety building in his chest like a balled-up fist. Like getting toothpaste back into the tube, he knew he couldn't unhear the information Dan was sharing with him. *What can I do with it? Am I supposed to do something with it?*

"If worldnewsdailyreports.com wanted to present some real research," Dan added, "they could have consulted Dr. Tom Horn, who has dug up actual reports from the Smithsonian archives that document the museum had found and studied ancient giant human skeletons in the past."

Dan quickly scanned the pile of blue folders and pulled one out from the bottom. "Here's an actual Smithsonian report titled 'Annual Report of the Board of Regents of the Smithsonian Institution Showing the Operations, Expenditures, and Condition of the Institution for the Year[s] 1873–1877.' Dr. Tom Horn, along with Steve Quayle and Tim Aberino, found the reports during their research. Some of the bulleted entries in the report are as follows. 'One skull measuring 36 inches in circumference—Anna, Illinois, 1873.'

"Here's another one. 'One full skeleton with double rows of teeth, buried alongside a giant ax,' referred to in the report as a 'gigantic savage.' And Amelia Island, Florida, 1875. Another example, 'One jawbone that easily slipped around the entire face of a large man on the research team. Kishwaukee Mounds, Illinois, 1877.' Why aren't those giant human bones on display in the Smithsonian?

"One of the main obstacles was John Wesley Powell. He became the first director of the Bureau of Ethnology at the Smithsonian in 1879, and he broadened the mission of the Bureau to include an ambitious effort to organize anthropologic research in America. The organizational program he created included his refusal to deal with the giant skeletons unless evidence could be discovered that proved where the giants originated from. He wanted to treat the whole topic as purely a matter of geology, and as a result, we don't know what happened to all the bones, but we do know not a single one has been displayed to the public."

Tim had been thinking, *I cannot believe how fired up I'm getting with this craziness. But it's beginning to feel like truth.* He interrupted. "With all due respect, Dan, he was one individual a century ago. There have been plenty of other officials at the Smithsonian who could have brought the giant skeleton finds to light if they actually existed."

Dan straightened his back and began to speak in a deliberate, unhurried manner. "Oh, there were others who continued to refuse to accept the evidence that didn't fit into their theoretical paradigms of human evolution and patterns of human migration." Dan rose from his chair and continued. "Aleš Hrdlička, during his time as the director of the Smithsonian, made every effort to steer the study of anthropology away from the massive amounts of evidence that showed a race of giants inhabited the Americas. He was known as the 'skull doctor' by Native Americans. He made sure evidence of giants was excluded during the thirty plus years that he directed and shaped the path of American anthropology. The countless newspaper articles document that the Smithsonian was notified routinely when giant skeletons were discovered in North America. Not one has ever been on display, much less studied and factored into man's understanding of the history of humans on the continent of the Americas."

"How many others share your view, Dan?"

"I think the correct answer is I share the view of a considerable number of established researchers who have published their findings, like Ross Hamilton, who wrote the book, *A Tradition of Giants*. As I told your father-in-law many times, I review the research of others and come to my own conclusions. In the case of giant humans, I'm convinced they existed in large numbers, and they were the Nephilim and their descendants."

"Do you think mainstream academia will ever confirm their existence?"

Dan shook his head. "Highly unlikely. The present-day effort to delegitimize the study of ancient giant human skeletons has come from many different angles—like we used to do in our deception operations. For example, there was an actual contest for people to create phony photoshopped images of ancient giant skeletons and win a prize for the best convincing fake photo! Now the fakes are being circulated on the web, and any real photographs are automatically discounted. The whole idea is to pollute the subject matter with garbage so that no serious-minded person will look into it and dig into the records to find the truth. Since it's been tainted by scandal and salacious falsity, now the average person won't explore the topic."

Tim frowned. "So, there's no independent evidence in circulation to support your beliefs about the true meaning of Genesis 6."

"Oh, there is. An excellent book by L. A. Marzulli, titled *On the Trail of the Nephilim*, documents that the Humboldt Museum in Winnemucca, Nevada, has four giant skulls locked up in their storage facility, but they aren't on display. Marzulli documents how a researcher, Pete Mansoor, had traveled to the museum and examined and photographed the giant skulls. When Mansoor asked a museum worker why the skulls were not exhibited, the worker claimed they couldn't be since they weren't recognized by the National Association of Museums.

"Another reason museums are reluctant to display giant bones in North America is the fear they are Native American and would be forbidden items, according to Indian tribes. Even so, some artifacts other than skeletons that are actually on exhibit in museums tend to show giants did exist in the past. For example, a giant ax head that is sixteen inches long and weighs twenty-seven and a half pounds is on display in the Creation Evidence Museum in Winnipeg. The giant implement was found near Swan Lake. The normal size for stone ax heads that have been found is roughly six inches long and about five pounds in weight. No normal-sized person could swing an ax with a twenty-seven-pound head with any accuracy."

Tim accepted a list of references from Dan.

"And there are some excellent books that document research into the topic. Take, for example, Fritz Zimmerman. He published an excellent work titled *The Nephilim Chronicles: Fallen Angels in the Ohio Valley*. Zimmerman does an exhaustive study of the burial mounds in Ohio. Steve Quayle and his associates have almost made a career of tracking down evidence of the Nephilim. Some of their best work is in South America and on the Italian island of Sardinia."

Tim stared at the sheet Dan had handed him. *Lord, please help me with all of this.*

Dan continued. "Other researchers are also finding evidence without realizing they're helping to confirm the existence of the Nephilim. Here's an example."

Dan scanned a sheet of paper and read: " 'New research shows ancient humans had sex with nonhuman species. A 25 July 2017 article in the *New Zealand Harold* reports that according to Omer Gokcumen, Assistant Professor of Biology at the University of Buffalo, ancients had sex with a ghost species or proto-human. The work was apparently based on DNA studies. Angels would be considered ghosts from the standpoint of a biologist. Other findings confirm that very unusual offspring have been discovered. For example, the elongated skulls found in Peru have only one parietal plate as opposed to two, which are found in humans.' Remember the Dan Aykroyd movie, *Coneheads*? Researchers are finding intact skulls that look exactly like a conehead. Very elongated skulls that are bizarre-looking and some still have red hair attached, with very large eye sockets. They clearly show an anomalous type of being that could have been the result of angelic breeding with humans. Normal humans have two parietal plates—plates that connect the front plate to the occipital, or rear, plate. The elongated skulls have only one parietal plate, which is a nonhuman trait. Some Peruvian children, whose heads were bound to boards by their parents in an apparent effort to mimic the elongated skulls, still have two parietal plates. The discouraging fact in all of this is that none of the findings I've cited are studied or taught in school. No wonder no one has ever bothered to consider the true meaning of Genesis 6."

Tim remained motionless for a few seconds and stared blankly into the room. After collecting his thoughts, he started to speak. Before the first word could come out of his mouth, his cell phone rang. He glanced at the screen and then turned to Dan.

"Sorry, Dan, I've got to take this call. ... Hi, honey, what's up? ...... They did?" Tim couldn't believe yet another disaster had befallen their lives. The church problems would have to wait. "Where? Okay, I'll be right there."

He ended the call and turned to Dan. "I'm sorry. My niece Julie was admitted to the hospital with a serious infection. She has a rare cancer of the bone marrow and can't fight normal illnesses on her own. I've got to be there."

"I understand," Dan said. "I'll pray for your niece. We'll pick this up when you're ready. Okay?"

"Sure, and thank you," Tim said while rushing out of the meeting room and before Dan could utter another word. "I'll be in touch."

Chapter 9
Sharpening Focus

Dan clicked the Save button on his home office computer before closing the Word document that outlined his marketing strategy. *I hope Ben is right.*

The new author realized the plan needed a lot more polishing before it was ready for submission to his targeted publisher, but at least now he had a draft. *I can't believe I've become one of those empty suits who tells stories for a living. I hate this whole idea.*

He got to his feet and stepped to the window. *But if it's the way to reach people with God's message, then I'll have to be open to sharing my past in a way that isn't about me. But how?*

After shutting down the computer, he swiveled his desk chair around and stared at the framed facsimile painting of Jesus Christ that hung on his office wall. While he gazed in awe at the image of the bearded Messiah, the vibration of his cell phone broke his concentration. He recognized the number.

"Hey, Ben, what's up?"

"I need your help. I want you to use some of your spook training to help me get some information on a person," Ben said.

"You mean my counterintelligence training?"

Ben chuckled. "Yeah, yeah, yeah, that spy stuff you know how to do. Will you help me or not?"

Dan laughed. While Ben liked to instruct others, he resisted being corrected by peers. Dan liked to take the opportunity to goad him playfully whenever he could. "All right, I guess I can. Who's the person and what do you want to know?"

Ben's silence made Dan think he'd lost the call.

"You still there?"

Nothing.

"Ben, I can't help you if I don't know what you want."

"It's about my former mistress, Nicole. My grad assistant located her."

Dan could hear the anguish in Ben's voice. *Oh, boy.* "I thought you parted company with her years ago. I remember your telling me the story in the airport. Frankly, I thought you were a heartless bastard when you told me how you sent that poor pregnant woman packing." Dan paused for a moment. "Did she have your baby?"

After a long pause, Ben spoke with a strained voice. "I don't think so. I mean, I'm not sure. I don't know, Dan. Whether she did or not, I need to tell her I was wrong and ask her to forgive me. I can't live with myself because of what I've done. I've got to make it right, and to do that I need to talk with her face-to-face."

"You said your grad assistant already located her. Why don't you go see her and say what you need to say? What do you need me to do?"

"I treated her horribly. I can't pick up the phone and call her like nothing's happened or go to her front door and start making small talk. She's a very proud and determined woman." Ben hesitated. "I'm sure she hates me. She'll hang up on me or slam the door in my face. I need to find the right place and time to approach her and try to get her to listen to me. It's important I don't do her any more harm, you know? I want a suitable location that won't allow her to run away. I have to know how she's living her life and who else may be part of it. I don't want to get assaulted by an angry boyfriend or fiancé. That's what I want you to do. Figure out her routine and decide the best way for me to approach her. I can't believe I have to tell you what I need. You should be telling me what to do—surely you've had your share of arranged meetings. I'll hire you, if money's the issue."

"Okay, okay, I get it. No need to hire me, that's what friends are for. But I want one thing in return. Remember how I told you I needed to go out on the speaking circuit? I want you to go with me when I try out one of my book talks. I want you to talk briefly about your NDEs."

"You've got it," Ben said, his tone lighter, almost eager. "Scout out Nicole for me first and let me try to right what might be the worst wrong I've ever done. Then I'll gladly go with you whenever you want."

"Deal."

***

The young man sliced open the top of a brown cardboard box with a box cutter and pulled out a large clear plastic bag of paper cups stamped with a round red-and-blue logo. The fluorescent light in the windowless storage room flickered for a moment as he shoved the heavy box back to the wall with his foot.

Turning to face the door, he heard the muffled sound of an intercom and the voice of a young woman ask, "Welcome to Burger Barn. Can I take your order?" through the thin walls of the cramped space. He hoisted the bulky plastic bag over his shoulder and pushed aside a white plastic five-gallon container of dill pickle chips with his other foot to clear his path.

Before he could turn the doorknob, the door opened and a young attractive brunette wearing a light blue apron over a red-and-blue uniform walked in and stopped, eying him with a direct gaze.

"You're new here," she said.

"Yeah. I started on Monday."

He felt awkward and glanced away from the imposing intruder. The young woman stood motionless and stared at him.

"I'm Susan." Her focus shifted from the young man's face, down to his nametag and then to his wrists and forearms, where there were scars of various sizes and shapes. Both wrists had a band of scar tissue around them.

"Looks like you've had a rough time. How'd you get all of those scars?"

The young man's internal guardian rose to the surface and answered reflexively. "Oh, I'm accident-prone. I played rough when I was a kid and have the battle scars to prove it." He turned away after his answer and headed toward the door.

"Wow, rough might be an understatement, but okay. It looks like we'll be working together tonight. Let me know if you need any help."

"Sure," the young man said.

Relieved to be out of the stock room, he headed back to the line to stock the cups holder. *I need a uniform with long sleeves.*

***

Dan strode into the bright and spacious Flagler Hospital cafeteria and perused the tables for a familiar face. He spotted Tim seated by himself, hunched over a tray of food. Dan went over and sat across from Tim, who was about to take a bite out of a generously garnished cheeseburger. Tim put the sandwich down on the plate and made eye contact with Dan.

"How's your niece?" Dan asked.

"Holding her own. They have her on antibiotics to fight the infection. And I've been wearing out the knees of my jeans praying for her. We're doing everything we can do. She's in God's hands now." Tim moved his burger aside, giving priority to the meeting.

"I'll keep praying too," Dan said. "I went by her room, and she was asleep. Liz told me you came down here to get some food."

"Yeah, I needed a break, and I wanted to talk with you away from everyone, anyway. I appreciate your taking the time to get back together with me. I've had some time to think about what you told me, and I agree I have a lot to learn about the Bible. We only got part of the big picture in seminary. But we live in a time when science is king, so everyone wants physical evidence to back up the written word. I believe you when you say it exists, but I don't have any idea how to find it. I'm losing my church, and I need some solid ideas on how to connect with the congregation and keep our doors open."

"Tim, you can make changes right away, without starting an intensive campaign to find evidence. I think the problem with people leaving your church may be even more fundamental. I suspect people are losing interest in your sermons because they think you're merely telling stories. They can't connect to them. They want more."

Dan inhaled slowly. "You can start with the New Testament since that's where the authors of the Gospel make clear their writings are their factual written testimony of what they witnessed and participated in. Like what a witness would write in a sworn statement for a criminal case."

"I guess I could take your approach."

"You can," Dan said. "Take the Book of Acts, for example. In chapter 3, Peter tells a crowd that he and his fellow disciples were all eyewitnesses of the life and works of Jesus Christ. When he's arrested by the Jewish authorities, he tells them he can't stop talking about Jesus' life, death, and Resurrection because he's simply telling others what he and his fellow disciples saw and heard." Dan leaned forward. Could he help Tim to see?

"They weren't stories. They were actual accounts that could withstand cross-examination on the witness stand. You need to drive that point home to get people to take the Bible seriously. They aren't fairy tales or myths. When people realize how alive the words are, they'll want to keep coming back for more. And, I suggest you stop referring to Scripture as stories. Use the term 'Biblical record' or 'Biblical account,' since that's what the Scriptures are."

Tim was listening intently, his frown replaced by an openness he hadn't had when Dan first sat down.

"You also need to draw on the events documented in the Bible to help your congregation get a better sense of how God thinks," Dan said in a soft tone. "That's why I spent the time explaining Genesis 6. People who skim parts of the Bible think God is a homicidal maniac. He's not. We're made in his image, so we think like he does, though in a much more limited way. We do things for a reason, and so does God. God doesn't do things arbitrarily, for his own satisfaction, or out of evil intent. He does them for legitimate moral reasons. You need to underscore that point. Human beings can't love someone if they don't understand them—that's all I'm saying. You have a lot of material you can draw on to make your sermons factual and captivating." Dan's voice was louder now. "When people sense you're telling the truth—the whole truth—including the supernatural aspects of the world we live in—they'll begin to appreciate your candor and honesty. You'll start filling your pews again."

Dan stopped. He was embarrassed about raising his voice. The passion he had for the message had carried him away. "All right, enough with my pontification."

Tim's laugh was shaky. He placed his hands palm down on the orange tabletop. "No, I need to hear this. I'm about to lose my church, and I need encouragement and passion. I admire you. You're speaking from the heart, which is rare these days."

Dan sheepishly surveyed the area to see if others had heard his impassioned impromptu sermon. When he realized the cafeteria was almost deserted, he relaxed and focused on Tim.

"Another thing you can do right away is to stop using 'Christianese' in your sermons. It turns people off and stops them from thinking. Ben could do a better job of explaining this than I can, but I think the best way to illustrate what I'm talking about is to use my past as an example. I came from a specific culture. People in the counterintelligence profession use specific words, phrases, and acronyms during informal conversations. They became a sort of verbal shorthand for us. We threw around terms like 'neutralize,' 'compromise,' 'OFCO,' 'terminate,' a 'dangle,' and so on. When you talk to your congregation, I recommend you use specific terms and get away from the Christianese phrases like 'I'm in a season' or 'I'm ready for a prophetic breakthrough' or 'a manifestation of an anointing on my life.' Those terms do have specific meanings, but for most, those phrases are vague and confusing. I think they actually cause the mind to stop deep thought. You want your congregation thinking deeply about God, and the best way for them to find him is to think about him without being distracted. While they think, they can begin to develop a relationship with him through regular prayers."

"Ouch, that hits close to home, but I believe you're right. I need to speak in clear language so people have clear thoughts."

"Exactly. As far as finding evidence to support the Bible, Ben can give you his take on my Apologetics 101 lecture. He was my captive audience in the Charlotte airport during the night when we were trapped together, so he got the full dose. When you can take a break from staying with your niece while she's here, we can get back to specifics. I know you can recharge your ministry and get your church on the right path. If you're interested, I could come in and speak during one of your services. I need the practice for my book business, anyway."

"Great idea. A real live NCIS agent who's found God! Let's do it."

Dan grimaced, but he knew Tim was right, although he hated hearing the words all the same. *I guess I've made a commitment I'm going to have to keep. I need to control my mouth. But it's time to start doing what I need to do.*

***

"Dr. Garvin, you have a visitor. He says you're expecting him."

The pretty young blond receptionist leaned into the doorway of the doctor's office while holding onto the doorframe. Her professional tone masked her unease. The doctor never received unscheduled visitors in his office late in the day, but this unanticipated caller was intimidating to her and he seemed uncompromising in a calm but determined way.

The smartly dressed ear, nose, and throat specialist turned away from his brightly lit rosewood desk and faced the receptionist. Before he could say a word, an imposing figure appeared behind her and stepped into the office.

The doctor, though startled, quickly regained his composure. "Thank you, Laura. I'll see the gentleman. You can go on home. I'll lock up."

The doctor closed the door behind his visitor.

"You're taking a big risk coming here," Dr. Garvin said. "A phone call would have sufficed."

"You know we can't discuss details of The Calling's business over the phone. You never know who might be listening. Besides, I wanted to deliver this message in person. I can't overemphasize how important it is for you to find the problem and take care of it. We can't afford to be exposed. I've told the coven to put a curse on him, but so far the seers can't tell where he goes when he leaves his apartment. That's why you can't fail. This kid is strong. He's resisting and reintegrating. And he's smart."

"I left the charged ring hidden on his sofa. He'll have his demon visitors. Maybe they'll drive him back to us."

The doctor paused and then made direct eye contact with his uninvited guest. "And exactly how did you get us into this mess in the first place? Why did you task a teenager to dispose of a body by himself?" Dr. Garvin asked.

"Emergency decision. One of our scouts spotted a deputy sheriff driving onto the property while we were conducting our Beltane ceremony. We had to do an emergency abort. Your target was tasked with taking the body for a ride and bringing it back for proper disposal after the heat cooled down. He never came back."

"You don't have your area under control. How could a deputy sheriff happen to drive onto your property during a ceremony?"

"The kid called in a homicide-in-progress right before the ceremony started. He used a throw-away phone, but we have the 911 call recording. It's his voice."

"How did you track him here?"

"Sources in our network. The target used his regular phone after he disappeared, and they triangulated his cell number to the neighborhood where you searched. It was the only rental property in the area. The idiot used his real name when he signed the rental agreement. We have our own people here in your backyard."

"Well, why didn't you use *them* to take care of him?"

"We needed someone with your special talents and respectable cover. Now you need to do your job, or we're all in danger. The kid's mind is clear enough for him to get us all arrested if he spills his guts to a clean cop."

"What are the chances of him talking?"

"Real good. He can call up any of his multiples at will. Don't know how he does it, but we know he can. His parents have been his programmers and handlers since birth, and they somehow screwed it up. They didn't update his programming before he left their home, so it's important you get to him immediately. We need to get to him before he gets to us. You know how to make it look like natural causes or an accident. Understand?"

"Perfectly. I'll take care of it. It'll be my pleasure. I may do it slowly and get a recharge in the process."

Chapter 10
Confronting Failure

Ben Chernick squirmed on the metal bench in the glass-encased Flight Bus Stop enclosure along North Twelfth Street in Philadelphia. The warm, muggy June air caused him to regret wearing a sport coat. He checked his watch: 1:25 p.m. Summer semester students streaming from the Samuel Paley Library headed toward the narrow asphalt road with trolley tracks in its center. As Dan had instructed, Ben pretended to be reading a newspaper he clutched as he peered across the tree-lined street.

Worried he was not performing his surveillance mission correctly, he referred back to the email of instructions that Dan had sent him. Ben dutifully watched an area north, across the street, as directed, toward the end of a row of take-out food kiosks with cream-colored stone facades and alternating solid red and red-and-white-striped awnings. Groups and individual diners were seated throughout two rows of more than a dozen permanent aluminum tables and benches installed in front of the kiosks. Food aromas hung trapped in the humid midday air of the enclosure.

Nervously glancing at his phone, he looked up periodically in the direction of the left end of the kiosks. Ben's attention was focused on the open area between the kiosks building and the multistory Gladfelter Hall, which housed Temple University's College of Liberal Arts. All of the restaurants in the small take-out cluster of kiosks were busy serving late lunchtime customers lined up to place orders.

While Ben watched the area where college students with backpacks strolled, a familiar figure caught his attention. A slim thirty-something female dressed in a dark skirt and white long-sleeved blouse made her way over to the Adriatic Grill and stood behind a couple placing an order at the takeout window. She ran her fingers through her brownish-auburn hair and turned briefly in Ben's general direction. Ben got a clear view of her face. He recognized the full lips, large blue eyes, small sculpted nose, and classic features.

Nicole! Exactly like Dan predicted. Man, he's good!

Within several minutes, Nicole turned from the food vendor and went over to an empty table and sat down on a bench with her takeout order packaged in a white Styrofoam container. Ben watched her begin to eat while she studied the screen of the phone she held in her left hand. Ben slowly proceeded in the direction of the restaurants and stayed out of Nicole's direct line of sight. He casually stepped behind her and circled back, and approached the empty bench opposite her. He remained silent while he sat down.

Nicole sensed the shadow cast by Ben and looked across the table to establish eye contact. She literally froze and stared at him. The fork in her right hand dropped into her food. After remaining nearly motionless for several seconds, she found her voice.

"How did you find me? Why are you here?" she uttered in a raspy voice.

"I'm sorry for surprising you like this, but I thought it was the only way. You're a hard person to find."

Nicole placed her phone on the table and stared at her lap. After appearing to collect her thoughts, she looked up at him. "And to what do I owe this honor? You come here after all these years and sit down while I'm having my lunch. Like nothing has happened. Never once did you attempt to find out if I was all right—if I was even still alive."

Ben grimaced; the truth seared his conscience.

"Oh, that's right. I was an inconvenience," Nicole stated. "I became a problem when I got pregnant. I interfered with your dignified life as a highly esteemed professor. None of your snooty faculty friends knew you were sleeping with your poor little grad assistant, and you did everything in your power to make sure our affair was kept a secret. I was in the way, and so was our baby!"

The word *baby* stabbed Ben's conscience like a switchblade. "Baby? You had the baby?"

"Yes, not that it's any of your concern. In all those years, you never once tried to contact me and find out how we were. And now you want to know about our child?"

Ben was gripped with a mixture of elation and stifling grief. Nicole's words crushed him with unbearable weight, yet brought him joy with the news of his child. He hung his head and talked softly. "I deserve every word you've said. I let you down. I abandoned you and our baby. I know this is awkward and very, very, late, but I'm sorry, Nicole. I'm not going to ask you to forgive me. I know my attitude and actions were unforgivable. Give me the chance to explain to you how I've changed. How my past has caught up with me and brought me here today. I'm a changed man, and I want to make it up to you and our child. I can't tell you how happy I am to hear you had the baby."

Nicole's jaw tightened. Her eyes squinted into a glare. She locked eye contact with Ben and spoke slowly and forcefully, almost as if she were speaking under her breath. "I'm gonna give you thirty seconds to get up from this table and leave, before I start screaming. Do you understand? Now leave me alone and never come back."

Tears welled up in Ben's eyes. "Look, I know I deserve this and a whole lot worse, but please give me a chance."

"Fifteen seconds."

"All right, all right."

Ben slid a business card onto the table and toward her as he stood. "My cell phone number is on the back if you ever change your mind and want to talk."

Nicole turned her head to the side and looked away with a scowl. Ben slowly backed away and left Nicole sitting alone.

***

The man in his early seventies, with thinning blond hair heavily streaked with gray, picked up the small stainless-steel bone-cutting forceps in his long, thin fingers and examined the new instrument's sharp edges. He found the Merced trademark he was looking for. *Ah, German made! Excellent quality.* After placing it on the blue paper-lined tray along with other instruments, he felt the cell phone in his knee-length white lab coat vibrate. He scanned the number of the incoming call and answered.

"Dr. Schmidt," the terse caller announced, "we have a problem with your son. He was given an assignment and didn't follow instructions. Has he contacted you?"

Schmidt's stomach tightened. He recognized the voice and knew there had to be a major problem for the person to be taking the risk of contacting him directly by phone.

"Not since he moved out on his own. He knows his limits and the consequences of not following orders. You must be mistaken. He would never do as you have said."

"Oh, he did, there's no mistake about it. And he made sure we knew he'd never come back. He was public in his act of disobedience. He exposed us all to great risk."

"If he did, you know what to do. Too much is at stake. But I warn you, he's smart and resourceful. You'll need to be very careful. I prepared him to respond to every threat. Find him and trigger his programming. He has many minders installed, and he'll get back into line. I can help you."

"It's too late. ... He already crossed the line."

Dr. Schmidt closed his eyes tightly and remained silent for several seconds. "All right, if you must take care of the problem now and can contact him by phone, use the suicide programming I installed. His termination code is 'Follow the yellow brick road.' But use it only as a last resort. You'll need to recover the body if you do, and I want it returned to me. Notify me immediately if you do the termination. Do you understand?"

The caller hung up. Dr. Schmidt locked his gaze on the operating suite's stainless-steel overhead light while he contemplated the ramifications of the phone call. He always knew this day would come—but not so soon. Despite the realities, he was saddened by the situation. *What does he remember and what will he do?*

Clenching his jaw, Dr. Schmidt turned his attention back to his phone, scrolled through some numbers, and hit Speed Dial. His nostrils flared as he glared into the brightly lit operating suite.

"Hello," a woman with a noticeable German accent answered.

"I warned you what would happen if we let him go," he whispered. "It's happened. His defenses and backup systems have failed, and he's beginning to reintegrate. I should have never listened to you. You thought we could maintain his programming through phone calls, but you were wrong. He knows better than to accept our calls, and the inevitable has happened. He'll never serve the brotherhood as an adult. Instead of helping him, you've done the opposite. Your weakness will cost him his life."

Dr. Schmidt ended the call and stormed out of the operating suite, slamming the door behind him.

Chapter 11
Second Chances

Ben had completed reading his Bible verses for the evening and was in the process of typing his daily journal entries when his cell phone rang and interrupted his concentration. He picked it up from where it had been sitting on top of his Bible and checked the screen.

He didn't recognize the number, but noticed the Pennsylvania area code.

"Hello?" he said cautiously. *Do I dare believe the call is from her?*

"Ben, it's Nicole," the female voice said. After a long painful pause, she uttered her first halting words. "I know I said I never wanted to see you again, but I've been thinking, and some things have happened. I wanted to give you a chance to apologize."

Ben felt a surge of joy and relief. "I can't tell you how happy I am to hear your voice," he said as he blinked back tears.

She said, "I was so shocked and upset when you sat down in front of me. You caught me by complete surprise. I'd written you off years ago. When I saw your face, it brought back all the bad memories."

Nicole paused. Ben could hear her take a deep breath and waited for her to go on.

"We've both hurt each other enough. It's time to act like responsible adults, so I want to hear what you have to say."

Ben pressed the phone to his cheek, closed his eyes, and thanked God. *It's more than I deserve.*

"I'm so glad you called. I deserved every word you said. I expected it, after the way I treated you. I've treated everyone in my life terribly, and now it's come back to haunt me. I've changed, Nicole. I'm not the same heartless creep you used to know. A lot has happened to me. I needed time to explain—in person. That's why I flew to Philly."

"I know. I'd just received some bad news related to us, and seeing you intensified my stress."

"News related to us? What news?"

"Our son."

"You have no idea what it means to me to hear you had the baby. You had a boy?"

"Yes. He looks like you."

Ben was ecstatic. "I want to know everything about him. What's his name? What's he doing now? Can I come to see him? And you, of course, you too …."

Nicole said, "I'm surprised you're so happy I had the baby."

"Yes, I've been trying to tell you I'm not the way I used to be. You were right when you called me a selfish bastard. I was only worried about myself and my position at school and what others would think about me. I never thought about how you felt. I didn't know how to consider other people's feelings. My wife divorced me when she found out about our affair, and I didn't do anything to try and save our marriage. I was too wrapped up in myself. Being a professor made me even more egotistical and self-centered. Plus, I had no faith. Then something happened to me and changed everything."

"You have changed. I never thought I'd hear you say that." Nicole stopped speaking and remained silent.

"That's what I wanted to share with you," Ben said. "Something has happened to me. I've changed physically and mentally. It's too complicated to discuss on the phone. I hope we can see each other soon, and then I can lay everything out."

The line was silent.

"Nicole? Nicole?"

"You need to know a few things," Nicole said. Her tone of voice changed, and she spoke in a quiet, flat tone.

"Okay, I'm listening," Ben said.

"After I stopped working for you and quit graduate school, I went home to see my parents to tell them I was pregnant. Like I told you would happen, they weren't happy. I was an embarrassment to them by being pregnant and not married. They're very old-fashioned in their views and outlook on life. Appearances and social standing are everything to them. When I told them you were Jewish, my dad became irate and ordered me out of the house. I was frantic and didn't know what to do, so I contacted my uncle in California. He and my dad had kept in touch with each other, and my uncle always liked me, so I reached out to him. When I told him my story, he and my aunt were sympathetic and invited me to come stay with them. They didn't have any children at the time. They encouraged me to have the baby so they could raise him as their own. Right before delivery, I told them about you. When they found out you were Jewish, their demeanor changed. They said they would adopt our son—but on the condition that I relinquish custody and never make contact with him again. They said they didn't want me to interfere with their bonding with him. I was so desperate, I agreed. After our son was born, I signed the adoption papers and never saw him again."

Ben was stunned, but he had listened without interrupting. He asked, "How long after he was born did you give him to them for adoption?"

"The baby was less than a month old. My uncle has connections, so he got the paperwork done real fast."

"Do you have any pictures of him?"

"Only one taken when he was a few days old. He has your dark hair and complexion, but he has blue eyes. He has a heart-shaped, wine-colored birthmark on the right side of his neck. Once I began to nurse him, my feelings changed and I wanted to keep him, but my aunt and uncle were adamant about the adoption and me leaving as soon as I could travel. I cried myself to sleep at night, but convinced myself I was doing the right thing for the baby. My uncle is a very wealthy surgeon, and they have a luxurious lifestyle. I didn't have anything then. My uncle put me in the hospital he uses and paid all of my expenses. I felt obligated to them."

Ben could hear Nicole softly sobbing and, for the first time in his life, he could feel someone else's anguish as well as his own. He silently mourned for her, for his son, for them all.

"What's his name?" he asked when her sobs subsided.

She sighed. "Keith. His middle name is Benjamin. My aunt and uncle wanted a different name, but I refused to sign the adoption papers unless they named him Keith. I know it was a mistake, but I wasn't thinking clearly at the time. I was so stressed out and afraid."

"Look, don't be so hard on yourself. You did what you thought was best for him." Ben stopped to compose his thoughts. He didn't want to betray his worry and anger with his voice. After calming himself, he continued. "Where is he now?"

"That's the problem. I lost all contact with my aunt and uncle. I used to call them periodically during the first few years after I gave birth. I called my aunt and got updates from her, but my uncle made it clear he didn't like me calling. He reminded me I had given up Keith through adoption and I should let him get on with his life without me confusing and upsetting him. My aunt assured me Keith was doing fine, so I didn't press the issue. I was busy with graduate school and, later on, getting a professor position at Temple, so I made the mistake of honoring their wishes and lost touch with them all."

Ben's stomach tightened. *Losing contact with your son? I feel your pain ....* "So, you've never seen him or talked to him since you gave birth?"

"Yes …. I know it sounds terrible. I'm so ashamed of myself." Nicole hesitated and then continued.

"Right before you came to Philly to see me, my uncle had called me, looking for Keith. I was shocked. I hadn't talked with him or my aunt in years and, out of the blue, they wanted to know if I'd heard from Keith. I'd honored their demand to not speak to my own child, and now they wanted to know if he'd reached out to me. When I asked them why they thought I'd know where he was, they said he'd moved out to be on his own and had broken off contact. They said they suspected he might have somehow learned about me. They were cold and brusque on the phone, and when I told them I had no idea where he was, they hung up. Needless to say, I'm really worried."

Ben was confused. His own behavior and selfish decisions had caused all this, but he had no idea how to fix it. Had he lost his son before he even found him? He was angry at the turn of events, even angrier at himself. He couldn't image how hard it must have been for Nicole, though.

He took a deep breath. "Look, the past is the past. Neither of us can undo the things we've done, no matter the reasons. The most important thing now is finding our son and making sure he's safe. We can both introduce ourselves to him at the same time."

Ben stopped for a second to consider how bizarre his statement sounded.

"All right. What do you want me to do now?" Nicole asked.

"I want you to put everything you know about Keith in writing and send it to me. The name and address of your aunt and uncle. The hospital where he was born … everything you can think of. I have a friend who's a retired NCIS agent, and he's an excellent investigator. He uncovered your daily routine for me."

"You mean you had him spy on me?"

"Not spy, just determine your daily schedule so I could approach you at the right moment. … Please trust me. He's good and he's on our side. Once you pull together the information on our son, I'll turn Dan loose. We'll find Keith, don't worry. I know he's fine."

"I hope so," said Nicole with a tinge of doubt in her voice.

I hope so too. My only son is missing ... what could happen next?

***

Connie Lucas handed grandson Aaron a small green plastic bowl of spaghetti as he sat at a white vinyl children's table in the middle of the kitchen. The three-year-old held the bowl tightly in his left hand while he eagerly shoveled in the last few bites with a child's plastic fork. His spaghetti-sauce mustache was growing by the second.

"Wow, you finished in a hurry. Do you want some more?" Connie asked.

Aaron aggressively nodded his head.

"All right, but this is your last bowl, okay? You ate a lot already!"

Aaron grabbed the bowl and shoveled in the fresh helping of spaghetti.

Holding a coffee mug, Dan strolled into the kitchen and surveyed the scene of Connie feeding Aaron. His heart swelled with love for his family. He treasured having his grandchildren stay at the house, particularly Aaron, his oldest grandson. Dan had bonded with him during numerous babysitting sessions. Aaron and his sister, Amie, had spent countless nights with Dan and Connie while their parents both worked to save for a house and build their careers.

Dan pulled a purple plastic child's chair next to the table and squatted into it to watch Aaron eat. He had to steady himself while he positioned his trim muscular frame on the small chair. Connie tended to the never-ending stream of dirty dishes that needed to be rinsed and placed in the dishwasher. Dan could smell the aroma of chocolate chip cookies baking in the oven. His wife loved to bake, and with grandkids around to feed, she could indulge her craving without feeling guilty.

"When will you see Ben again?"

"We're going to get together next week and go over a book presentation I'm working on. I want his part to be dramatic, but he's resisting me. He said he'd go out on the speaking circuit with me, but he's been occupied with other things and hasn't made himself available. I understand, though. He's been through a lot and now wants to get his life back together. He patched up his relationship with his daughter Ruth, but now he has to repair his relationship with the mother of his child, who refuses to speak with him. He's under a lot of stress. I'm trying not to add any more."

"How's he doing with his son?" Connie asked.

"He's never met him and thinks he may never have a chance. He's very depressed about it. I told him—"

Dan was cut off in mid-sentence by the ring of his cell phone that was charging on the kitchen countertop.

"Speaking of the devil—" Dan recognized the number of the incoming call and answered.

"We were just talking about you."

"I'm sure it was good," Ben said, and chuckled. "I've got some good news and some bad news for you. Can you talk now?"

"Never too busy to talk to you. What's going on?"

"Nicole called me."

"She did? Great. Looks like your effort to reconnect may be paying off."

"In more ways than one. She apologized for rebuffing me in Philly and wanted to hear me out. I couldn't blame her. At least she didn't slap my face there at the table."

"Outstanding news."

"Yeah, but that's not all of it. That's the good news part. She also wanted to fill me in on what was going on with our son." Ben stopped, then cleared his throat. "Seems he never lived with Nicole, and now he's disappeared."

"What? … Are you kidding?" Dan couldn't believe what he was hearing. Poor Ben.

Ben explained how Nicole had contacted her aunt and uncle out of desperation, and ended up having the baby and turning him over to them through adoption.

"Nicole said it seemed like the logical thing to do at the time, and since she was in such a state of distress, she agreed to their terms, thinking she was acting in the best interests of our son."

"I understand," Dan said. "Adoption is a good option for a lot of families."

"I know you're right, but they forbid her to be part of his life. Since Nicole lost contact with Keith, she had no idea what he was doing, but she assumed he was well cared for by her aunt and uncle. Her uncle is a pediatric surgeon and quite wealthy. Her aunt is a concert violinist. She always assumed Keith would have the very best in life. Everything changed shortly before I approached Nicole. She got a call out of the blue from her uncle, asking if Keith had contacted her. It seems Keith left home and now they needed to recontact him for some reason, but couldn't find him. Nicole thinks something is wrong and is very worried. She asked me for help in finding him, and I naturally thought of you."

"Thanks for small favors." Dan laughed. "I'm the guy you come to when you need to be bailed out."

"Will you help me find Keith?"

"Let me see. You still owe me your esteemed presence at an upcoming book talk, and you've made zero progress on your part of the presentation…"

"You're right. I need to get busy, but I can't focus now. I'm too distracted by Keith's disappearance. Please help us find him, and I'll do ten book talks with you."

"All right. But I'll hold you to ten talks. Agreed?"

"Agreed."

"Okay. I need you to get as much information as you can from Nicole about Keith and her uncle and aunt."

"Already done. I'll shoot you an email with all the details in a few minutes. You're a lifesaver. I owe you."

"You always do. I'll get back to you after I look over the information. Now, stop worrying. We'll find your boy."

Dan put the phone down on the counter and turned toward Connie, who had stopped her kitchen work to listen in on Dan's side of the conversation.

"Another trip?" Connie asked.

Dan heard the resignation in her voice. He'd spent most of their marriage traveling without her, and he'd promised those days were over.

He rested his hands on her slender shoulders and pulled her gently to him. "Another trip. Only this time, I have no idea where I'll end up."

Chapter 12
Secrets from the Past

Dan took one of the last remaining aisle seats near the back of the plane on the crowded flight—the only acceptable option for him. After flying armed as an NCIS special agent for almost a decade following 9/11, his old habits were hard to break. He wanted the freedom of movement in the event of a disturbance, and it gave him the vantage point to eyeball all the passengers coming onto the plane. He couldn't relax on a flight, even if he had long since turned in his badge and gun.

While he watched his fellow passengers slowly shuffle down the center aisle and struggle to squeeze their carry-on bags into the packed overhead bins, he caught a glimpse of an individual who grabbed his attention.

A middle-aged man, with thick salt-and-pepper hair combed straight back and a salt-and-pepper beard, appeared overdressed in a blue herringbone tweed jacket over a button-down dress shirt. A heavy silver chain with a silver crucifix hung around his neck and rested on his shirt mid-chest. He inched his way down the aisle, scanning the rows for an empty seat.

Dan had hoped he could keep his row all to himself to spread out, but he realized his wish was futile; the flight to Portland, Oregon, was going to be nearly full. He continued his scrutiny of the passengers and saw the impressively dressed man make brief eye contact. Within a minute, the man was within a row of Dan's seat, and as the gentleman fixed his gaze on the empty window seat in

Dan's row, Dan heard something that brought back a flood of memories.

"Is that seat taken?" the man asked Dan while pointing toward the window.

Dan recognized the heavy accent—Russian.

"Nope," Dan answered flatly, and stood to allow the man into the row. Dan had switched into protection mode.

After the man sat and secured his seat belt, he hoisted a black leather attaché case onto the middle seat between him and Dan. The rather expensive-looking case had the worn outline of an odd-shaped emblem embossed on the top. Curious, Dan tried to use his peripheral vision for a better view of the unusual symbol. He was able to make out a round shape with some sort of figure in the middle. Straining his eyes to see to the left while barely turning his head in the same direction, he was able to discern what appeared to be the image of a man on a horse, slaying a dragon with a spear.

Hmmm, what could that mean? Dan decided to memorize the image and research it later, when he was alone.

The Russian pulled out a phone and started scrolling through messages, ignoring Dan, who had removed the Kindle from his backpack and jumped back into an e-book.

At least he's quiet, Dan thought. After several minutes of trying to read during the constant drone of flight announcements and the mandatory safety briefing, he closed his Kindle and looked out the window, past the Russian, as the plane accelerated and climbed into the cloudless blue sky. The plane completed its ascent and leveled off at cruising altitude. The Russian, who. had stowed his attaché case for takeoff, removed it from under the seat in front of him and placed it back on the empty center seat.

Dan glanced at it again and saw a clearer view of the embossed emblem.

"I like your briefcase," Dan said, surprising himself.

Without changing his expression, the Russian answered, "Thank you."

"That's an interesting emblem," Dan stated as he stared directly at the case. *Why not ask? He's obviously not trying to hide it. I wonder what he'll say. He's wearing a crucifix. Maybe he's a real Christian.*

"Do you have an interest in symbols?" the Russian asked.

"Some symbols, particularly ones I've never seen before. Some believe symbols have a certain power. I'm not sure I agree, but I like learning about them, particularly ones that deal with spiritual topics."

After the word 'spiritual' left Dan's lips, the Russian turned and studied Dan's face. After doing what appeared to be a quick evaluation of the American stranger who had an unusual curiosity, he glanced down at the case.

"The briefcase was a gift from a former colleague. The symbol is actually the image of a sketch drawn by a fellow countryman. It's called 'Light Conquers Dark.' The artist was Nicholas Roerich. Have you heard of him?"

"Can't say I have."

"Roerich was a painter, writer, and an archaeologist. At least that's how the public knows him. He was also a theosophist. Do you know what a theosophist is?"

"No, not really." Dan was surprised by the Russian's openness and articulate speech. Although the Russian had a thick accent, his command of the English language revealed a highly educated man.

"Theosophy is a religious philosophy that another one of my fellow compatriots, Helena Blavatsky, brought to the United States during the late nineteenth century. She taught that an ancient secretive brotherhood of spiritual masters existed. She believed the masters could tap into the power of the spirit world, and she was on a mission to resurrect the brotherhood. Roerich studied her teachings and initiated his own search for the secrets of knowledge and paranormal powers. He believed the masters were attempting to revive the knowledge of an ancient religion once found across the world and which would again come to surpass the existing world religions."

Dan was shocked at the man's openness.

"Sounds like he was into the occult."

While retaining a stoic expression, the Russian continued on as if he were giving a college lecture. "That's a rather harsh characterization, but it's essentially true. Some claim it has its roots in the Christian Bible."

"Hmm. What parts of the Bible refer to an ancient religion based on the occult?"

"Are you a Bible scholar?"

Dan laughed. "No, I'm not a scholar, I'm more of a student. I like to dig into the Bible and get to the true meaning of the passages. I think most people read it and don't understand what it says. I'm trying to put what I've learned into a book I'm working on." Dan stopped talking. *Too much information.*

"I see. The Bible talks about ancient gods who came to earth and taught man many things, like astrology, metallurgy, engineering, and other facets of higher knowledge."

"And what parts of the Bible contain this information?" Dan became ill at ease as the conversation continued. The information the Russian was discussing sounded familiar, but he couldn't relate it to a specific book of the Bible.

"It's contained in extra-biblical texts like the Book of Enoch, and it's referenced in many books of the Bible, but it really starts in Genesis 6."

The words from the Russian's mouth hit Dan like a sledgehammer. *Of course. Why didn't I make the connection? I can't believe I sat next to someone interested in the very passion of mine. I need to pick this guy's brain!*

"What a coincidence." Dan tried to keep a cool exterior and not reveal his excitement. *What are the chances?*

"I'm extremely interested in Genesis 6," he said. "I think it's one of the most misunderstood and understudied parts of the Bible. It seems you've made some additional connections between the Old Testament and the history of man."

The Russian opened his briefcase, retrieved a card, and handed it to Dan. "Here is my private number. If you believe God is the source of all power in the universe, and then you see others who crave power but claim it comes from another source, you must study them and be on guard. Their actions and goals can ultimately harm you if you take no action. There is no middle ground.

"Ms. Blavatsky and Mr. Roerich spent their lives searching for the sources of counterfeit power in the dark corners of the universe, when its source, our Holy Father, was at the very bright center. Dark powers, at least while the world is intact, can be used to inflict great damage, particularly if they are used by people in positions of world governance."

Dan took the card and studied it. The card displayed the name Vladimir Smoilov and a phone number in the center—nothing else. *This is not a chance meeting. We're both interested in how man uses the occult for a source of power. What are the odds of sitting next to this man?*

"Thank you." *Why is this man so open with a stranger?* "I suspect you don't give your card out often. I'm Dan Lucas, by the way."

Dan extended a hand, and the Russian shook it with a strong grip. Not usually so forthright with his personal information, Dan regretted his decision to reveal his name; on a deeper level, he felt he had made the right decision.

"You are correct, Mr. Lucas. But I've never met a stranger interested in the book of Genesis the way you are. You revealed who you are by revealing your hunger for truth." The Russian paused a moment. "Were you aware there is a Nicholas Roerich Museum in New York City?"

"No, I wasn't."

The Russian leaned toward Dan and began speaking in clear but hushed tones. Dan had to lean forward to hear.

"You Americans—if I may say—have a weak grasp of your own country's history. But I understand. Some important events in one's country are purposely ignored or misrepresented. It seems your press has been taking lessons from my former country, where the news is used as a tool and frequently a weapon. Many of your universities are not much better."

Dan liked this man, but was becoming uncomfortable talking with the surprisingly talkative Russian within earshot of total strangers. He felt compelled to keep his plans and beliefs private. Fortunately for Dan, the muffled roar of the plane's engines served as a sound-masking device.

"Other than being an artist and a student of the occult, why is he important to the US?" Dan asked. "We have plenty of home-grown followers of the occult right here in America."

"Nicholas Roerich was a mentor to one of your Secretaries of Agriculture, who served under President Franklin Roosevelt. You probably carry a symbol with you that was the result of Roerich's influence. Apparently, some members of your government had a relationship with Russians long before it became fashionable to brand every contact an act of espionage."

Dan chuckled. "Good point. What symbol are you talking about?"

"Do you happen to have a one-dollar bill with you?"

Dan pulled out his wallet and sifted through the bills. He pulled out a one.

"May I see the back, please?"

Dan complied, and the Russian leaned over and pointed at the bill.

"Your country celebrates the constant flow of immigrants to your country as a source of strength. They are, and I consider myself one of them. But sometimes, foreigners bring beliefs with them that may have unintended consequences. Take your one-dollar bill." Pointing at the back side, the Russian said, "Do you see the pyramid and the banner below with the words, *Novus Ordo Seclorum*? Do you know the meaning?"

Dan felt a twinge of embarrassment. He hated not knowing everything—a byproduct of his old world of dealing in a hypercompetitive government bureaucracy and a remnant of his pride he constantly battled. He controlled his emotions and focused on his aisle mate.

"Can't say I do."

"The Latin translation is 'New Order of the Ages.' Some interpret the meaning to be the 'New World Order.' "

Dan felt his stomach tighten. *Oh no, not a conspiracy theory nut! He was making so much sense, and now this! ... He seems smart, though .... If I listen, I might learn something new.*

"Notice the eye on the top. Some would argue it signifies the eye of Providence or the eye of God watching over humanity. Others would say it's the All-Seeing Eye, used as an official Masonic symbol. Still others say it's the Eye of Horus, which is actually the Eye of Satan. Regardless of what it stands for, the question is: Why would such a controversial symbol be placed on the currency of the United States and who would allow such an act?"

"Good question," Dan said. "Who put it on the dollar bill?"

"The symbol was placed on the bill during the administration of President Franklin Roosevelt. Who was responsible? Nicholas Roerich. Through his relationship with Agriculture Secretary Henry Wallace, who was deeply involved in the occult, he used his influence to see the symbol placed on your currency and, ultimately, your President Roosevelt approved its use."

Dan recoiled. He'd never considered anything related to the occult could be connected with the US government—a government he had served faithfully for many years. The thought that a satanic symbol could have been secretly placed on the US dollar shocked him.

"I had heard something similar, but I never took any of it seriously. After all, this is a country based on Judeo-Christian values."

"You should take the research of others whom you trust seriously. You Americans call yourselves a Christian country, but where are all of your Christian symbols?"

Now Dan felt more ill at ease. "On our churches," he replied. "Almost every town or city has at least one Christian church with a publicly displayed cross."

"But how about your government buildings?"

"They're not allowed to have Christian symbols anymore."

"But you have plenty of pagan and occult symbols, starting with your currency."

"I'll grant you those symbols are troubling, but I doubt if most Americans pay much attention to them. No one looks at a dollar bill anymore."

Dan didn't believe his own words and chided himself silently after making the statement. He'd spent considerable time researching the power of symbols, and now he sounded like the shallow naysayers he had grown to detest.

Smoilov stated, "You said yourself that symbols related to spiritual matters have power. But symbols play another, equally important, role that most ignore."

"Like what?" Dan asked.

"Displaying symbols repeatedly in public serves a purpose. First, occult and new world order groups follow a code of conduct that compels them to put their symbols in plain sight so they can serve as a warning to the astute that they are active. Secondly, the continual display of a symbol is the first step in conditioning the public to accept it. You display a symbol often enough and as widely as possible, like, for example, the logo of an energy drink, and you desensitize the public to it, regardless of its real meaning. Then it becomes familiar, and ultimately, the public develops an unconscious fondness for it because of familiarity. That's a very important step, if the symbol stands for something evil."

Dan felt deflated, depressed, and conflicted. He deserved the mini-lecture from the Russian since he'd betrayed his own inner beliefs by using careless language for the sake of making conversation. He also didn't like hearing information that undermined his perception of his government. If fight or flight were his only options right now, he was ready for flight. The coward's way would be to change the subject, but how, without looking the part?

"It sounds like your Mr. Roerich did some damage, if what you say is true," Dan said.

"He wasn't the only one. Your country has a fixation on Russia for political purposes, but there have been influences from others far worse than Russia."

"Like who?"

"Think back to recent history. At the end of World War II, my country swallowed up large parts of Eastern Europe and made them a prison camp. But your country suffered as badly, in a much less obvious way. Cancer usually starts on the inside of the body and often isn't detected until the patient is near death. You deliberately brought some disease-carrying agents into your own country—all in the name of national security. Yes, you advanced your country's national defenses, but you paid a heavy price that virtually no one knows about."

"I'm not following you."

"At the end of World War II, your country brought in thousands of Nazis to help with your space and national defense programs. But with them, you brought an evil that could not be seen with the naked eye. Yes, some of the lucky Russians who could escape Stalin's grasp made it here too, but the Germans—many former Nazis—brought a spiritual sickness that infects parts of your society, even today. A sickness that remains hidden from view."

"You're saying the German scientists and academics brought into this country were all into the occult or lovers of Satan?"

"Not all, but some, and enough to do damage, particularly the physicians. Most Americans don't realize that occultism was central to Nazism. No one adequately screened the brilliant German scientists and medical doctors for undesirable traits or beliefs that could pose a threat to society. Almost all of them were Nazis. I understand how it happened—you can't read people's minds, but you did have a military and civilian counterintelligence structure that could have done a much better job of screening your émigrés and kept out those who brought a spiritual cancer with them, a cancer that was at the core of Nazi beliefs. Those doctors who worked in the concentration camps performed more than standard medical research. They learned how to enslave the mind while the body remained free."

"I was never taught about any of this in my history classes."

"That wasn't an oversight. Your government didn't make public what it was doing, so most Americans are unaware. If you're concerned—and by your expression, I would say you are—I suggest you research the subject for yourself. At least you can find out what evils simmer under the surface in your country and are starting to emerge."

"I appreciate the history lesson. I guess I've got some work to do. Thank you."

The Russian nodded and turned back to his phone.

Dan leaned back and took a deep breath. His mind reeled. *I need to do some digging. A lot more digging.*

Dan closed his eyes and replayed what Vladimir had told him. This particular man choosing to sit next to him was no more of a coincidence than when Ben had taken a seat next to him in the Charlotte airport. It was part of his journey and deep inside he knew it. *Will I have what it takes to find this hidden evil and, even so, will I know what to do?*

He thought he probably knew what David must have felt like when facing Goliath.

Chapter 13
Staring into the Abyss

Dan maneuvered into the St. Augustine diner's compact booth and laid his ball cap on the thickly upholstered vinyl bench seat. He was pleased Ben had requested a booth at the far end of the diner, away from prying ears. Ben was already seated, with a glass of ice water in his hand, and looking eager to talk. The chatter from the mostly middle-aged lunch crowd provided a steady din of background noise in the tube-shaped stainless steel–clad structure. A complex aroma of cooked food drifted through the air.

"Glad to see you made it back safe and sound," Ben said with an expression of concern. He hesitated for a moment and continued. "I wasn't able to sleep last night. When you told me you didn't want to discuss what you'd discovered in Portland over the phone, you got me real concerned." Ben paused, staring straight at Dan. "So how *did* it go?"

"It took longer than I expected, but the trip was very enlightening. Got a chance to see some old buddies on the West Coast and catch up." Dan stopped when the waitress came and took their orders.

"You said you may have some answers about what happened to my son. I'm all ears," Ben said.

"Yeah, I didn't locate him, but I think I know why he left Nicole's aunt and uncle and went out on his own. It took me a lot of digging before I got anything solid. This case has been a real education for me. If I hadn't had some NCIS friends who knew the area, I wouldn't have been able to make the connections I needed. I struck gold when I was introduced to a retired detective who has a case file on your son's adoptive parents. He's keeping his notes in case some solid evidence surfaces that could lead to a prosecutable case."

Ben opened his mouth and stared at Dan. "Are you kidding me?"

Dan shook his head, leaned forward, and spoke in a quiet monotone. "When we finish our lunch, we need to take a walk down to the plaza so we can have more privacy. What I'm going to tell you isn't pretty."

Ben froze momentarily, his glass in midair, and kept staring. "It's that bad?" He placed the glass down.

Dan looked around and noted no one was seated near their booth. After his visual sweep, he got down to business. "I don't know how to break this to you, Ben, but I think Nicole's uncle Klaus and aunt Helga abused your son."

Ben closed his eyes and swung his head back until he faced the patterned aluminum ceiling. He remained motionless, with his eyes squinted shut. After nearly a minute, he leveled his head and opened his eyes. "I don't know if I can take this, but I have no choice," Ben said breathlessly. "I have to know the truth if I'm ever going to be able to help him." He paused and stared at the table. "Go ahead."

"Your information about Nicole's aunt and uncle was accurate," Dan said. "Their address in Portland, Oregon, was correct, as was all the other info Nicole gave you. But that wasn't the half of it. Klaus and Helga are full-blooded Germans from the old country and, evidently, they can't tolerate those with 'impure blood,' if you get my meaning."

"I assumed Nicole had German ancestry by virtue of her family name, but I never gave it a second thought, and she never talked about it," Ben said.

"Apparently, family lineage and ethnic background are very important to Klaus and his family."

"Now I'm starting to see why they reacted the way they did when they found out I was Jewish. But I don't understand why they agreed to adopt Keith after knowing he was fathered by a Jew," Ben said.

"That's where the problems start for Keith, unfortunately," Dan said. "Newborn infants are highly sought after in Klaus and Helga's demented world. They wanted to use him in their evil secret life for a specific purpose … and, by the way, Nicole doesn't have one uncle, she has two. I don't think she knows about the second uncle, Hans."

Ben nodded once and replied, "She never mentioned him, so you're probably right."

"Anyway, Nicole's father, Peter, and his two older brothers, Hans and Klaus, were born before World War II, in Nazi Germany, and your son's adoptive father was the oldest of the three. They grew up in a fiercely anti-Semitic family near Munich. But what was most significant for Ernie, my new detective friend, was that they came from a specific Bavarian bloodline that was suspected of being part of a group called the Illuminati. The full name of the organization is the Order of the Illumined Wise Men, or the Ancient and Illuminated Seers of Bavaria. Anyone born into the family was to be raised in a very specific way that ingrained in them total submission to the Order, from birth. Family members believe that by reason of their royal ancestry, they're chosen to become part of a ruling elite who will eventually form a consolidated world government. They believe they have not only royal lineage, but also a hidden occult heritage that traces all the way back to evil supernatural beings from biblical times. Their vision for the future includes eliminating hundreds of millions of undesirables from the world's population to make ruling more manageable and the planet more sustainable."

Ben looked incredulous. "Do you believe that? Sounds like lunatic fringe nonsense."

"I didn't believe it before, but I do now—at least parts of it." Dan slowly nodded. "What's more important is they believe they should and will do it."

Ben squinted his eyes and pursed his lips. Dan recognized his disbelief. He continued on.

"Some of the details may be wrong, but I think the core facts are accurate. Ernie gave me a crash course on the Illuminati and related groups, their systematic abuse methods to create controllable subjects, and the new world order. Some of the abuse is actually torture, and parts of the conditioning involve satanic rituals. Drugs and hypnosis are also staples of their program. He also introduced me to a Christian therapist, Trish, who helps victims of satanic ritual abuse recover. One of her clients claims to have escaped from the Illuminati and is living in hiding under an assumed name. Trish was a treasure trove of information."

Dan halted and stared straight at Ben with a look of all business. "Like you, I always considered it to be nonsense dreamed up by tin-foil-hatted conspiracy theorists in their advanced stages of paranoia, but now—"

"Dan," Ben said in a loud voice, "how could a professional like you get sucked in to believing such garbage? The Illuminati is an urban legend created by the entertainment industry to sell music and keep the feebleminded masses entertained. If you want to learn about the Illuminati, turn on MTV and listen to the lyrics of some of the rap videos. A lot of my undergrads listen to that nonsense. And the satanic ritual abuse hoax was debunked decades ago, when the stories about daycare center abuses broke. Don't you remember? Shrinks looking to make a name for themselves invented repressed memories, and soon kids were remembering all kinds of bizarre events that were planted in their minds by the people who were supposed to be helping them. I can't believe you'd fall for such rubbish." Ben's face reddened and the veins in his forehead were noticeably engorged.

Dan shifted mental gears. As he would during an intense interrogation with a difficult subject in his NCIS days, he controlled his emotions and forced himself to stay focused on the facts.

"Take it easy, Ben," Dan said in a slow, firm voice. "Remember how I told you in the airport last year that I never believe anyone and always assume people are lying? I haven't changed. I take everything with a grain of salt. In this case, I spent hundreds of hours in libraries and in my hotel room reading books and searching the internet. After I found numerous unrelated references that contained essentially the same information, I realized I should take what Ernie and Trish had to say seriously."

Ben relaxed his shoulders and leaned forward while he clutched his condensation-coated glass of water. He stared blankly at the off-white tabletop and then shifted his gaze to Dan. His response was calm and measured. "Yeah, I remember what you told me, and I think I know you well enough to accept what you say is true." Ben stopped speaking and glanced at the table before looking up again. "But how in the world did this detective come up with all this information?"

"Slowly, over decades. Ernie became the go-to guy in his department for any cases related to the occult and Satanism, and as his reputation grew, his bosses sent him to conferences and symposiums. He made a lot of contacts, and after he established his bona fides, fellow professionals shared information with him. He then took his knowledge and proceeded to develop informants and insiders. Many were former victims who had escaped their tormentors. He met Trish while working a case. She herself was a former victim of satanic ritual abuse before she became a therapist. She's used her experience in dealing with real satanic ritual abuse cases to help Ernie better understand the problem. He's built up his knowledge base to the point that he can speak with authority. I must have spent a solid week with him, picking his brain and firing questions at him. He always had an answer and the evidence to back up his claims, and during the few times he didn't know the answer, he was honest about it.

"He could be all wrong, but since others have come to the same conclusions separately, I don't think so. He's met my burden of proof. I'll always be alert and continue to ask questions, but until he proves otherwise, I consider him a reliable source."

Ben exhaled slowly and leaned back against the bench seat. After remaining silent for a moment, he said, "All right, I guess I overreacted. The thought of Keith being abused is more than I can handle right now. And then you say Nicole's aunt and uncle are part of some sort of evil aristocracy that plans to take over the world. It's too much to take in at one time. You can understand that, can't you?"

"Of course I do. It wasn't easy for me, either. When I was first introduced to Ernie, I thought he was a nut job. I don't think so now. Same for Trish. I consult with her on information about the methodology of different satanic groups. But one thing I'll never stop doing, I'll always keep vetting information and looking for deception."

"Okay, okay, I understand, but please explain to me exactly how one goes about taking control of the world," Ben said, his trademark sarcasm oozing to the surface.

"Gradually, over many generations, by the subtle steering and manipulation of elements of the international banking system, the targeting of key components of international organizations like the UN, the cooption of key officials in governments of sovereign nations at every level, the insertion of loyal curriculum administrators in the education system, the infiltration of churches, the subversion of the entertainment industry, and, most definitely, the recruitment of members of the media. The secretive elite who want to rule are extremely wealthy, and they've used their billions to manipulate people over the centuries. They operate as both respectable citizens in public view and as the personification of evil in secret.

"The group considers themselves Luciferians and not Satanists, but it's really a deceptive tactic to mislead others, particularly the lower-level members of their various groups who think they're serving a greater good and an actual being of light. When you learn who and what they worship during their rituals, you have no doubt they're satanic. Powerful demons like Baal and Moloch are not loving entities of light and love. The Illuminati and other satanic cults call on demonic power to help themselves reach their collective goal."

Dan took a sip of water, then dropped his volume a little more. He wouldn't risk embarrassing Ben. "You were in the presence of demons in hell, Ben. You know they exist and can exert great power over humans in the supernatural realm or in our physical world, in some cases, too. The elites, for centuries—starting with the Egyptians—learned how to make contact with the demonic world and draw supernatural power from them. Once they learned how to summon Satan and his henchmen, they perpetuated their practice of seeking power through the worship of the evil one and preparing select members of each successive generation through trauma-based mental conditioning and behavior modification."

"It goes all the way back to the Egyptians?"

"Yep, they serve as the inspirational roots for several groups. Aristocratic Europeans for centuries have viewed early Egypt as a utopian society and a model for a Luciferian world civilization. The Illuminati and other groups model some of their practices on those of the ancient Egyptians."

"And Nicole's family was part of it?"

"Yes. They were born into it. Klaus' father, Helmut, was a physician who ended up working at Auschwitz under Josef Mengele. Since Helmut was a product of multigenerational structured abuse from his own family, he took naturally to the horrific practices of the Angel of Death. Most people know Mengele for his barbaric experiments on concentration camp victims, but what most people don't know is he also perfected an organized process for trauma-based behavior control, through trial and error on helpless Jews. I know it sounds farfetched, but I believe he survived the war and went on to continue his evil activities for decades. There's a long trail of evidence that clearly points to Mengele's post-World War II activities in Germany, South America, and North America."

"I don't believe that!"

"I don't have direct evidence, but I've read multiple accounts from actual victims of trauma-based behavior control programs here in the US. They described Mengele to a *t*. He went by aliases. Some knew him as Dr. Green, others Dr. Black or Dr. Swartz. Ernie found declassified documents that detailed how Mengele was captured by US forces in Germany in 1946, and then, according to the French, he was released without explanation."

"I've never heard this," Ben said. "I thought Mengele had escaped to Argentina after the war, and died there."

"Some say he came to the US, and I can't prove otherwise, but I believe he may have been working with a select group of our government under the guise of national defense. Our government apparently believed his trauma-induced behavior modification program, which results in the subjects developing dissociative identity disorder, was a necessary evil that was needed as a defensive tool to counter the Communist threat during the Cold War. The US Senate's Church Commission held hearings on the program in 1975 and developed much evidence, even though CIA Director Richard Helms had most of the program's files destroyed in 1973. Mengele's monstrous brainchild actually existed, but the CIA ended the official program, known as Project MKUltra, and its offshoots around the time of the hearings."

"Official program? You say that as if there's some kind of an off-the-books program still operating," Ben said.

"Victims of similar programs continue to come forward even today, so some element of the program survived at least into the '80s and probably beyond. I don't think it's part of an authorized US program today, but I think an offshoot has been continued in secret. Ernie believes it's a program known as Monarch, and billionaire Illuminati members are funding and operating the program through subordinate programmers who received their training in government programs decades ago. I'm sure you've heard of the book, *The Manchurian Candidate.* Mengele was helping individuals in our government produce assassins who would kill and then not remember their mission. Remember the Jason Bourne movies with Matt Damon? Hollywood re-created their own version of the trauma-based behavior modification program for the big screen. The movies may seem like pure fiction, but they're based partly on fact. It's a whole separate field I'm starting to get my head around, but back to your son and how he was pulled into a life of abuse."

Ben rubbed his eyes and took a gulp of air. "Do you think he's still alive?"

"I do. He's apparently very strong-willed and determined. Ernie thinks Keith's life was spared when he demonstrated as a child that he had a very high tolerance for pain and could handle the torture and obey commands. Ernie also thinks he may have displayed a high IQ as he matured and was considered a potential future leader in the Illuminati. His leaving his parents leads Ernie to believe he has the will to live and to be free, rather than be a robotic servant of the satanic elite."

"He's like his old man," Ben said. He instantly regretted his attempt at halfhearted humor when the thought of his son's suffering came back to mind.

"You might be right. You showed me in the airport last year that you have a strong will to live. Your heart attacks would have killed most people. I think your son got some of your survival genes." Dan paused. "But I think he got his IQ from his mother."

Ben laughed, but his face revealed worry. He paused and tilted his head. Dan waited. He'd give Ben time to start to digest his disturbing news.

"If Nicole's uncle Klaus left Germany, why did he continue in his sick practices into adulthood, while living here in America? Did he still think he was destined to rule the world?"

When Ben posed his question, a pretty college-aged waitress arrived with their orders. She set a large salad bowl heaped with greens and strips of turkey, ham, and cheese in front of Dan.

The sheen of the grilled rye bread of Ben's Reuben gleamed under the diner's overhead lights. Ben stared at the sandwich like he had no idea what it was. "I'm not sure I can even eat now. How will we find him, let alone free him of these people?"

Wish I had a solid plan, buddy. Dan shrugged slightly. "We'll find a way. And we'll need to be fortified to do it, so eat up. You're wasting away to nothing," Dan said with a forced grin. None of this was funny, but he couldn't let Ben go insane with worry, either.

Ben looked dubious, but picked up the sandwich and raised it in a mock salute. "I guess you're right. Here's to success," he said wryly.

Dan nodded and dug into his salad. "When we're done, we'll go for a walk."

***

Connie Lucas shielded her eyes from the intense midday Florida sun while she pulled open the white metal mailbox door and grasped a thick stack of folded mail. One envelope made of heavy stock paper protruded from the usual assortment of advertisements and pleas for money. She stood at the curb and performed her usual ritual of separating the items destined for the recycling bin from the real mail. She pulled out the utility bill and the richly textured envelope from the stack and placed them on top. The Lerner and

Steele Publishing return address on the beige-colored envelope caught her attention. Her heartbeat quickened. Dan would be extremely interested in the letter. *Is it good news, I hope?*

When Connie closed the mailbox, she felt a wave of unease sweep over her. Walking up the long concrete driveway, she mused: *He shouldn't be getting a letter from the publisher this soon. They're still waiting for his marketing package before they make a decision.* Connie sensed the letter would not be welcomed news for Dan. She hoped she was wrong as she closed the heavy burgundy front door of the house.

She placed the stack of mail in its usual location on the kitchen counter, where Dan would sift through the pile and pull out his magazines and letters. Connie took care of the bills—a family routine they developed after decades of Dan being gone on NCIS missions and Connie being left to handle the household in his absence.

She picked up her cell phone and started to dial, but stopped.

Maybe I shouldn't bother him with possible bad news. He'll be home soon enough. On second thought, I know he'll be upset if I don't let him know the letter arrived.

Connie pulled up Dan's number and stared at the screen.

Chapter 14
Digging Deeper

Dan Lucas scrawled his name on the credit card slip and placed it in the black check holder. After sliding his wallet into the back pocket of his cargo shorts, he looked across the table at Ben.

"Ready?"

"Ready," Ben said. "This is your turf, so you lead the way."

Dan guided his friend down the concrete ramp of the polished steel diner and to the corner of Malaga and King Streets. Turning left, they strolled past a series of historic buildings and quaint residences until they reached Flagler College. Ben stopped to admire the unique Spanish Colonial Revival architecture that was accented with intricate Moorish trim.

"This place is amazing! No wonder you like exploring here," Ben said while examining the majestic cluster of buildings.

"Yeah, if you wait here long enough, you might see Harry Potter leave the building."

Ben laughed while still gazing at the lush enclosed courtyard and ornate terra cotta–trimmed towers that framed the sprawling structure once known as Henry Flagler's famed and luxurious Hotel Ponce de Leon.

"I've never seen a college like this!"

"It is one of a kind. Flagler built it in 1888. Some say it was the first hotel to be wired for electricity when it was constructed. Did you know Flagler imported Tiffany stained glass for the windows of the dining room?"

"I had no idea."

"They're worth over two hundred fifty million dollars today, and the inside is spectacular too—it's like a fine museum. Ever heard of George W. Maynard? He painted the murals in the rotunda and the dining room. He's the same artist who painted the incredible murals in the Library of Congress."

Ben stared in awe as they crossed the street across from the high-end multistory Casa Monica Hotel, with its Spanish-themed architecture.

"What a place … so beautiful and so rich in history."

"You've got that right. This is why Connie and I moved here. The weather's not too bad, either," Dan said with a grin.

The two men continued eastward, toward an expansive open plaza that appeared in front of them. To their left was a stately two-story building that had an old-world feel. Dan pointed to the structure.

"The king of Spain addressed the city from the balcony of this building during St. Augustine's 450th anniversary in 2018. It's the Governor's Quarters, which was used during the colonial days by the Spanish, and later, the English," he said.

Dan guided Ben across the street, to the main promenade filled with regal live oaks, palm trees, assorted obelisk monuments, and concrete walkways and benches.

"The pathway we're on now is the Andrew Young Crossing. We're in the Plaza de la Constitucion, the oldest public park in the United States. This walk commemorates where Andrew Young marched in June of 1964, at the request of Dr. Martin Luther King Jr. Young and his marchers were attacked by a group of thugs, and the assault helped galvanize public support for the passage into law of the Civil Rights Act."

"I could spend weeks here," Ben said. "You're living near a historical gold mine."

"It is. Connie and I never get tired of roaming around this beautiful town. We almost always discover something new."

Dan spotted an empty concrete bench shaded by a huge live oak. To their right, across the street, stood the Trinity Episcopal Church built in 1821, and to their left, across the plaza, was the Cathedral Basilica, built in 1793, based on a congregation formed in 1565, the oldest operating Catholic congregation in the United States.

"Let's sit here in the shade. We'll have some privacy."

Dan observed the widely scattered groups of tourists strolling through the plaza in the bright noonday sun. A constant breeze from the nearby Matanzas Bay provided some relief from the heat and humidity.

Satisfied no one was within earshot, he said, "Now, back to your question at the diner. Why do I believe Klaus stayed involved in the Illuminati when he left Germany with his mother? One reason, he had no choice. At his young age, he was still dependent on his mother for total support. She controlled his life."

"But why would he continue in the Illuminati and practice Satanism when he got older? You said his brothers Hans and Peter didn't continue in the family, as you call it."

"For one main reason, I think. The behavior modification programming his father inflicted on Klaus, starting at birth, ingrained in him the need to obey orders without question. He was taught that the torture he had to undergo was for his own good. Pain is pleasure and pleasure is pain. Ernie suspects Klaus' father told him what he did to him was because he loved him, and all the training was going to lead to his spiritual enlightenment."

"Disgusting," Ben interjected, "but it makes sense. Klaus conditioned him to need to stay with his mother and her fellow abusers. Almost like the Stockholm syndrome, where the captives develop a loyalty to their captors."

"Exactly. Since Klaus was the oldest of the three sons, his parents Helmut and Bridgette subjected him to structured trauma for the longest length of time. His mind conditioning was more firmly installed. Nicole's second uncle, Hans, was subjected to abuse for a much shorter length of time while he was very young, and the chaos of the war in Germany prevented his tormentors from continuing their work.

"By the time Nicole's father, Peter, was born, in 1944, Helmut was a doctor serving the Third Reich, under Mengele in Nazi-occupied Poland. He wasn't home and available to administer the structured abuse program to Peter, and the other trainers working in the family were also drafted into supporting the Nazi military."

"So, Nicole's grandfather, Helmut, probably never abused Nicole's father, Peter?"

"Probably not. Helga may have initiated some structured abuse at birth, but she was probably preoccupied with surviving while Nazi Germany crumbled into ruins around them."

"What happened to Nicole's grandfather?"

"Based on his own research, Ernie believes the Russian army captured Helmut in Poland when the war ended. He was never heard from again, so most believe he was either killed or died in a Russian prisoner-of-war camp. Bridgette managed to escape from Germany and make her way to America with her three sons. Nicole's father, Peter, and his middle brother, Hans, got separated from their mother after they arrived in America and ended up in an orphanage, but Bridgette was able to retain custody of Klaus and keep his programming intact. Other wealthy members of the bloodline living in Pittsburg, Pennsylvania, took care of Bridgette and Klaus, which included resuming the traumatic abuse and indoctrination of him.

"When Klaus became a teenager, the family paid for him to go to medical school, like his father. Ultimately, according to Ernie, Klaus and Helga, who were maneuvered into an arranged marriage, moved to the West Coast, where Klaus became the head of the local Illuminati Council in the Portland area."

"Why didn't Klaus' family stay together when they got here in the States?"

"I don't know. Ernie thinks the mother may have had problems with US immigration because her husband was a member of the Nazi Party. He believes she voluntarily put Nicole's father and his other brother Hans in an orphanage when she was about to be deported. Ernie also thinks Illuminati members in the US pulled some strings at the last minute and got Bridgette and Klaus visas."

"Hmmm. I would think a Nazi would have had a tough time immigrating to the US, especially the wife of a Nazi war criminal," Ben said.

"You would think so, but Ernie believes there was an even darker motive for Bridgette to make sure she retained custody of Klaus and not her younger sons. The break in the training of Hans and the virtual lack of training of Peter made them far less suitable candidates for roles in the family, and Ernie thinks that was part of her decision to release them to US social services. Nicole's uncle Hans was adopted by a devout Christian family, and he lost contact with Nicole's dad, who was passed around to different foster families. They both learned later in life that older brother Klaus was in the Order, and out of fear, they isolated themselves from the family and from each other. Ernie suspects Nicole's parents never acknowledged the existence of Hans or the family's Illuminati history."

"So, how did Nicole know about her uncle Klaus if her father and uncles all separated once in the US?"

"After Klaus became a successful pediatric surgeon, he established a routine of sending money on a regular basis to Nicole's father, Peter. Not sure why, but he ensured they stayed in contact. Ernie believes they never actually visited each other—they only maintained sporadic contact through letters. Ernie guesses Klaus sent money to Nicole's father to buy his loyalty in case he needed him for something in the future."

Ben opened his eyes wide and raised his eyebrows. "This is unbelievable. How in the world did this detective come up with all this detailed information on Nicole's extended family?"

"Ernie kicked off his career-long mission when he was still on the police force. A woman came into his department and filed a complaint about Klaus. Ernie took the report. The woman alleged that she took her six-month-old son to see Klaus to have his inguinal hernia repaired. When she found out the surgical fee was far more than she could afford, the doctor suggested she allow Klaus and Helga to adopt the child and give him a good life. The woman was a poor Hispanic single mother with a limited income and no insurance. After she said no, he became more insistent and hinted he could turn her in to Immigration Services, thinking she was in the country illegally.

"She left the office and reported that Klaus had threatened her and wanted to take her child. When Ernie investigated the case, Klaus denied the threat, and since it was a he-said-she-said case with no independent evidence, Ernie had to close the investigation as unresolved. While Ernie was doing the case, he dug into Klaus' background and found out he had initially been trained as a plastic surgeon, but later trained to be a pediatric surgeon. An odd career change, in Ernie's opinion, but one that put Klaus in contact with a lot of children. Ernie later met Trish, who had a client who claimed she had escaped from the Illuminati and implicated Klaus in satanic activities. After Ernie developed enough information about Klaus and his past, he convinced his boss to let him travel to Germany, where he tapped into a tight circle of occult investigators and historians who had a lot of information on the Schmidt family. They welcomed an American police officer who was respectful of their country and willing to listen and learn. Now, Ernie has volumes of information waiting to be used in a trial."

"So one case led your friend Ernie into a career of investigating satanic crimes?"

"Yes. He was so appalled at what he was learning about the Illuminati and people like Klaus, he took a personal interest in pursuing similar cases."

Ben shook his head and momentarily closed his eyes while he contemplated Dan's information. "Did Ernie ever produce any concrete evidence that proves Klaus is a Satanist?"

"No direct physical evidence, but he did take me out on a short surveillance of Klaus' residence. It's a mansion on a big piece of property in a secluded area. We went in on foot through some woods and got a good view of the home in the late evening. Ernie pointed out the house has a full basement with windows painted black and covered with bars. He told me he'd been able to track down the contractor who built the house and confirmed the basement has two levels. Klaus told the builder the sublevel of the basement was going to be a wine cellar, but the contractor never installed any of the equipment you'd normally need, like a temperature control unit or wine racks. He did install a lot of sound deadening insulation on the basement's upper level for what Klaus claimed would be an audio-video studio for making medical training films.

"Ernie believes the subbasement is a satanic temple where Klaus conducts his ceremonies, and the upper level is an Illuminati training room, which is, in reality, a sterile, high-tech torture chamber. Ernie observed a large number of cars at the property at various times and even traced the license plate numbers back to individuals who were all pillars of the community. He thinks he knows who's in Klaus' Illuminati Council brotherhood, but he can't prove anything."

"I'll go in there and kill the SOB myself," Ben shouted.

Several tourists strolling nearby turned at Ben's outburst and hurriedly guided their small children away from where Ben and Dan were seated.

Ben's face reddened. "Guess I better tone it down," Ben said in a meek tone. "I can't understand how all this could have been going on in Nicole's family without her knowing about it."

"You'd be surprised at what people do in their private lives that you don't know about," Dan said. "One thing I learned from Ernie is the Illuminati are extremely secretive and have excellent operational security. Probably as good as some of our intelligence agencies. Information is shared on a strict need-to-know basis."

Ben shook his head and looked at his watch. "Can we take a quick break? I need to find a restroom and buy a bottle of water. This heat's drying me out."

"Go ahead. I'm fine," Dan said. "I'll save our bench while you're gone."

***

The young man hoisted the heavy duffel bag into the car trunk and slowly closed the lid. He scanned the immediate vicinity to see if anyone had noticed him, and when he was confident he was not being watched, he opened the driver-side door and eased into the car. He turned and surveyed the bedding and pillows in the back seat and then glanced over one more time at the second-story apartment that had been his home for months.

With a sense of grief and anxiety, he started the car and slowly drove away. He checked the rearview mirror constantly, until he got out into traffic on the main highway and blended in with the other cars. When he determined no one had followed him, he relaxed. Time to go to work.

***

"Man, my head is spinning," Ben said as he sat next to Dan on the concrete bench in the plaza. Dan clicked off the screen of his cell phone and watched Ben reclaim his seat in the shade of the decades-old live oak.

"Here, I brought you a bottle of water," Ben said. "I still remember when you gave me a Coke in the airport last year, when I took the seat next to you at the departure gate. I was trying to ignore you. I thought you were a nosey pain in the neck, but when you gave me a drink, I decided you were probably an okay guy."

Dan laughed. "Are you kidding me? I was thinking of changing seats! I thought you were a pretentious stuffed shirt who was straight out of left-wing central. If you hadn't answered me and started to lighten up, I would've been out of there."

They both laughed, but Ben's laughter quickly faded away. His pain and concern were etched into a frown.

"I don't know how you kept all the information you collected in Portland straight in your head. I expected you to bring some of your infamous blue folders with you today. You memorized a lot of information."

"It's not hard to do when it's such an intense topic. Remember, I've spent the last few weeks immersed in this stuff," Dan said.

"Okay, so explain something to me. You said Klaus didn't leave his mother when he got older since he was conditioned to obey. I assume his mother, Bridgette, is now dead. What's keeping Klaus going today? His mother isn't around to give him orders, and he has the money to live a normal life."

"I think, in addition to developing subpersonalities to survive the abuse and not lose his mind, he was later trained to abuse others. Ernie thinks he developed perverse needs that could only be satisfied by inflicting pain on trainees. When you're a victim all your life, anything that'll give you a sense of power and control can be therapeutic."

"But he could still stop if he wanted to, couldn't he?" Ben asked.

"Harder than you think. At the very core of the extended Schmidt family is a pervasive evil that infected Klaus. Demons and evil spirits took advantage of the evil acts perpetrated by the family as entry points into each member of the family. The sinful acts gave the demons a legal right to take up residence in them, almost like a form of partial possession. Outwardly, the signs of demonization are extreme narcissism and psychopathic behavior."

Ben had an astonished look on his face. "I want to know why they singled out my son for abuse when they adopted him," Ben said. "They had the resources to fulfill their sick needs before Keith came along."

"You're right, they're rich, but Klaus and Helga were never able to have children—at least not children they officially recorded as born—and they were limited to obtaining children from other council members. Some of the women in the council were strictly breeders who gave birth to children who wouldn't be sacrificed. They also needed a supply of children who weren't going to be trained, but simply used during satanic ceremonies and, in some cases, sacrificed. Ernie thinks Keith's availability as a newborn was probably considered an unexpected gift for Klaus and Helga, and since Keith had some royal lineage through Nicole's side, Klaus made an exception and decided to prepare him for a role in the family. Ernie believes Klaus hid Keith's part-Jewish ancestry from the ruling family."

Ben wiped his face with his handkerchief, hung his head, and closed his eyes. After remaining silent for a long moment, he focused on Dan. "What about Nicole's parents?"

"I think after her dad realized he came from an evil family, he turned to an ultraconservative Christian church to compensate for his past. I suspect his church concentrated only on the word of God but didn't apply it with love, so people were shunned who had out-of-wedlock births or similarly perceived moral failings. Her father didn't want to be humiliated in front of his fellow church members by admitting his daughter had been living in sin. He was so deeply scarred from his childhood and his family's past that he couldn't think clearly to put Nicole's interests first."

Ben opened his mouth and stared at Dan. "How did Keith get away from Nicole's aunt and uncle?"

"We don't know. Ernie believes Klaus may have been grooming Keith to go on to medical school and become a doctor by day and an Illuminati leader by night, but something must have happened. Keith may have shown signs of rebellion, so Klaus changed his programming from medical school scholar to a failing student dropout who had no hopes of college. After Keith turned eighteen, he somehow convinced them to let him leave home. Ernie thinks Klaus, like most Satanists who have dominated their victims with systematic abuse since birth, was so arrogant and overconfident of his ability to keep Keith's programming intact by phone calls and text messages that he had a lapse in judgment. Ernie suspects Keith cut himself off from all contact and has begun the process of reintegrating his multiple personalities and is healing."

"Where was he headed when he left home?" Ben asked.

"Not sure. We think he concealed his true intentions by telling Klaus and Helga that he was seeking out another Illuminati-connected satanic coven to join in another state. Most likely, Klaus and Helga knew the high priest in the coven he was joining. Although some of Keith's alter personalities were apparently still able to direct him while he interacted with the coven, his core personality was starting to reintegrate and he was searching for someone he could trust who would help him. Ernie thinks Keith never knew Nicole was his birth mother and that he was adopted, but he did learn about the existence of his uncle Hans somehow. Hans is actually living up the road from us in Ponte Vedra. Go figure. I think Keith may be on his way here to try and contact him. Maybe he's hoping to get help."

"How can we locate Keith?"

"I'll contact Nicole's uncle Hans and alert him that Keith may try to contact him. In the meantime, I need you to stay in touch with Nicole and keep us informed about any contact from her aunt and uncle. But don't tell her about Keith's abuse. We need to go to

Philly and break the bad news to her in person. She'll pepper you with questions, and you'll need my help with the answers."

Ben nodded.

"Maybe Tim and Ruth can help too," Dan said.

"Ruth doesn't know anything about this yet," Ben said. He looked down, paused, and resumed speaking as if he were a criminal confessing to a crime.

"She has no idea she has a younger brother. Once I find him, I want to bring him with me to Ruth's house and, ultimately, back to Pennsylvania to keep him safe. The poor kid's gonna need some major healing after what he's been through."

"You've got that right. He'll need the right kind of therapy from someone who knows how to deprogram multiples. He may also need some drug rehab. My biggest concern is that he may suffer from demonic oppression and be filled with anger and rage."

Ben buried his face in his hands and remained still. The bell from a tour trolley clanged in the background. Dan looked at Ben's mostly gray hair and remained quiet while his friend silently grieved for the plight of his son.

Eventually, Ben straightened up, rubbed his eyes, and turned toward Dan. "You know, when you hear about the sick and demented actions people take, you have to ask yourself why. What motivates these people? Is it really evil that makes them worship Satan? Or is it greed that makes them want to rule the world?"

"Good question," Dan said. "I think people like Klaus and Helga have an end game. They believe that if they give their full allegiance to Satan, are obedient to the point of making a blood oath with him and committing unspeakable evil acts in his name, they'll rule in hell with him after they physically die. You and I both know that's a lie, but they believe it. They think they'll be gods in hell, like they are on earth. They have no fear of hell. They look forward to it. And you know better."

Ben shook his head vigorously. "These people need to be stopped. I don't know much, but I do know that no human rules in hell."

As Dan nodded, his cell phone rang. He glanced at the screen and back at Ben. "It's Connie. I need to take this."

Ben nodded.

Dan said, "Hi, hon." ...... "What? ...... Hmmm. Interesting. I can't understand what they'd want at this stage, but I'll be home soon." *This is probably not the news I was hoping for.*

"Everything okay?" Ben asked.

"Not sure. Connie said I got a letter from my publisher. I wasn't expecting one. Let's call it a day and I'll get you back home. I'm a little distracted right now."

Ben, sensing Dan was troubled, gestured with a thumbs-up.

"There's more I need to tell you," Dan said. "It's disturbing, but you need to know it all."

Ben closed his eyes and nodded. He felt the energy drain out of his body when he thought about hearing more bad news about his son. He wondered when it would end.

Chapter 15
Setbacks

Dan picked up the heavy envelope that Connie had neatly stacked on the kitchen counter, on top of the other mail. He pulled out a one-page letter and forced himself to start reading. His stomach tightened as the words on the paper smothered his mind like a heavy piece of wet canvas.

Dear Mr. Lucas:

In reference to our telephone conversation regarding your proposal for *Life Begins with Death,* I regret to inform you that after further internal consultations, we must withdraw our conditional offer for publication. Our marketing department has determined that you lack the basic elements of a functional marketing program, and further efforts to pursue publishing your submission would not be in the best interests of Lerner and Steele.

Should you develop a viable marketing platform to support the publication of your proposed book, please contact Ms. Denise Anderson at the number listed below. She will assess whether you've made sufficient progress in your marketing efforts to warrant reconsideration of your manuscript package.

Sincerely,

C. R. Benson

Dan dropped the letter onto the countertop and closed his eyes. He felt like he was under a tsunami of defeat. *I took too long to get back to them. I should have known better. They thought I wasn't serious.* After saying a short silent prayer, he stared straight ahead.

I want to quit, but I can't. I can't let God down. I've got to get the truth out. Time is running out.

***

Early lunch hour traffic on the picturesque section of Florida's State Road A1A was starting to pick up when Dan pulled into the parking lot of the upscale Ponte Vedra office complex. Dan read the building's office numbers after briefly glancing at the address on his phone.

The neatly trimmed landscaping and rustic stone exterior gave the commercial complex a chic look. He found office number 421 and proceeded to enter through the heavy mahogany door that bore the sign H. S. SCHMIDT, CPA in gold lettering. On the right of the main hallway, a woman in her early forties was seated at a desk in a small office.

"Can I help you?" she asked.

"Yes, I'm Dan Lucas. I have an eleven thirty appointment with Mr. Schmidt."

The woman looked down at the appointment book and back at Dan, who was dressed in khakis and a light blue short-sleeved dress shirt. She gave an approving smile.

"Yes, Mr. Lucas. Mr. Schmidt will be with you in a moment."

Dan sat in a brown leather armchair with thick upholstery and dark mahogany armrests. He temporarily relaxed while he stared at the dark walnut hardwood floor and tried to clear his mind.

When thoughts about the conversation he was about to have slowly drifted into his consciousness, his heart rate increased and a telltale tightness filled his chest, so he shifted into a determined mindset. After Dan had been waiting for several minutes, the intercom on the woman's desk phone buzzed. She put the phone to her ear and looked in Dan's direction.

"Mr. Lucas, please follow me."

She escorted Dan to a large, plush office lined with framed certificates and degrees. Dan surveyed the office as he always did when he entered a room. He noted an elegant brown leather couch and several chairs around a small conference table with a rich, dark satin wood finish. He didn't see any exterior exits—something he made a mental note of—and then he turned his attention to two large overstuffed armchairs arrayed in front of a large mahogany desk covered with neat piles of folders. All of the items on the desk were precisely arranged in order, as if an engineer had measured the desk and carefully calculated where each item had to be placed, down to the perfectly aligned collection of pens.

A tall, slim man in his mid-seventies rose from his chair behind the desk and leaned over, with his right hand extended.

"Hans Schmidt. Please have a seat."

The man was pleasant, but his voice had a layer of tension and strain that betrayed his attempt at being welcoming. Dressed in dark charcoal gray dress pants and a burgundy-and-white pinstriped button-down shirt, the man was a few inches shorter than Dan. Alert and agile for his age, Hans Schmidt sat down. He was meticulously groomed. His neatly combed short white hair framed a lean, lined face with a sharp nose, strong chin, light blue eyes, and perfectly trimmed white eyebrows.

"What brings you here today, Mr. Lucas?"

"I'm considering starting my own publishing company and wanted to get some insight into the tax implications of running my own business."

"I see. Are you an author?"

"I am, but I'm new to the business side of writing. I've finished my first book, but can't seem to find a publisher who'll put it into print yet. Since no one else seems to want to take a chance on my work, I'm considering publishing it myself."

"All right, a typical small business to handle the type of work you have in mind would best be served by a limited liability company, or an LLC. They're relatively easy to set up and not cost prohibitive. We would be able to create one for you, if you're interested. Once your LLC is established, your business expenses and income would pass through to your personal return."

"Sounds promising. I'll seriously consider one."

Schmidt swiveled his chair around until he faced a bookcase behind his desk. Every file and folder in the bookcase was arranged with precision. He pulled out a thick glossy folder with an "H. S. Schmidt CPA" logo on the front and handed it to Dan. His facial expression was flat.

"You'll need to complete this package before we can establish your LLC. Once you've assembled the needed documents, come back in, and we'll finalize the creation of your company. If you decide to hire any employees for your business, we can help you set up payroll and some accounting procedures to help you keep your company running smoothly. Is there anything else I can do for you?"

Dan paused, collecting his thoughts. The appointment had moved along much quicker than he had expected. Schmidt was a man of few words. Dan detected a slight German accent. *He must still speak German at home.*

Dan stared at his feet for a moment, and then spoke. "Actually, there is, Mr. Schmidt. Forgive me for mixing business with a personal matter, but someone's life may be at stake."

Schmidt stiffened in his chair and fixed his gaze on Dan. The mood in the room changed drastically.

"Oh, really? What's the nature of *your* personal business that brings you into *my* office?"

"Mr. Schmidt, I'll get right to the point. The daughter of your younger brother, Peter, became pregnant eighteen years ago while she was still single and a graduate student. The father of her child was her boss, a college professor. Your brother Peter, and his wife, Karin, declined to help their daughter, Nicole, because they were embarrassed about her having a child out of wedlock. Nicole desperately needed support, so she contacted your older brother, Klaus, and his wife, Helga. They agreed to help Nicole, so she moved temporarily to Oregon to live with them and give birth to the child."

Schmidt slowly closed his eyes tightly and leaned back in his chair. He remained motionless as Dan continued to reveal the story he could now recite in his sleep. He decided to skip the background information and get to the heart of the matter.

"You know your brother Klaus is a Satanist, don't you, Mr. Schmidt?"

Schmidt opened his eyes and stared at Dan. While remaining motionless, he said, in a low monotone voice, "How did you get this information, and why are you here telling me this?"

"I got the information, Mr. Schmidt, through an investigation I conducted on behalf of the father of Nicole's child. I conducted the investigation to try and locate a young man whose life may be in danger. Your nephew, Keith. He may be on his way to Florida right now to find you. He's been abused all his life, and he has no one he can trust. He thinks his mother is Helga and his father is Klaus. He has no idea he's been adopted by his aunt and uncle, but he does know he has another uncle. You."

Schmidt said, in a rushed whisper, "I-I-I can't believe this. My family is evil. You have no idea how deep the evil runs. There's no civil way to describe their horrific way of life. I don't want anything to do with them."

Schmidt stopped. His voice was quivering with emotion. He pursed his lips and peered straight at Dan. "My parents created a living hell for us and dragged my oldest brother down with them. I don't know what happened to Peter when we were separated, but if I had tried to contact him, I would have exposed myself and my family to Klaus and that evil witch who called herself my mother. I mean 'witch' in the truest sense of the word, Mr. Lucas. Did you know my father was a physician who conducted medical experiments on defenseless prisoners in Nazi concentration camps? He deliberately infected inmates with typhus and yellow fever to test experimental vaccines that never worked. Those people died slow, horrible deaths. He deliberately placed adults and children in ice baths and watched them slowly freeze to death while he soullessly recorded the amount of time it took for them to die. He bought into the black flame of Germany before the rise of Hitler because it aligned with his own vile and wicked upbringing. He brought blackness and evil into our family, and he and my mother inflicted it on my brothers and me."

Dan felt the immense emotion behind Schmidt's words and forced himself to remain still. In a low tone, he said, "I understand he had a very dark past."

"My father was evil to the core. I was only exposed to him as a child, but I remember the look in those dark eyes. Evil, pure evil. One minute he'd be kind to us and give us toys and pets like a kitten or a puppy, and then he'd slaughter the poor animal right before our eyes and warn us that if we didn't follow his orders, we'd suffer the same fate."

Dan shook his head and forced himself to compartmentalize. He couldn't afford emotionality right now, or he'd lose Schmidt and the help he could afford for Keith.

"Do you know what it's like, Mr. Lucas, to lie in bed and cry yourself to sleep? To be consumed by crushing fear day and night? Fear of something you don't understand? It wasn't until years later, in this country, that I fully understood why my mother and father would literally keep me in a cage during the day and take me out at night like an animal. They'd wake me up in the middle of the night. They were wearing black robes and took me into a room full of hideous adults who'd commit horrific acts of abuse on me while my parents held me down. After the torment, they'd pretend to be kind to me and tell me every evil act they did to me was for my own good. Do you know what it's like to be consistently traumatized as a young child, Mr. Lucas? I do—it happened to me. I still have night terrors. No, Mr. Lucas, I'll not be drawn back toward that evil. I was blessed to have been separated from that monstrous woman when we escaped to this country, and I never want to be near her or anyone else associated with her in any way again. Am I making myself clear?"

"Crystal clear, Mr. Schmidt." Dan paused while he mentally recovered from Schmidt's jolting confession.

"But keep in mind," added Dan, "that your nephew Keith is just as desperate to escape that evil as you are to remain free of it. He may come looking for you because he has nowhere else to go and knows of no one else he can turn to. I'm sure you'd have done anything to find a caring and loving adult to rescue you from your parents, and he's now probably trying to do the same."

Schmidt slumped in his chair and began to speak while looking down at his lap. His voice was flat and barely above a whisper. "Someone called me a couple of months ago and addressed me as uncle. It sounded like a teenager or a young adult. Since I know some in my family are still involved in witchcraft and demon worship, I thought it was a trap. I hung up."

Better than I hoped! "You did? I need his number."

"I deleted it. My family and I have been terrorized by the black royals ever since we moved here. Their enforcers come up to me in parking lots and whisper veiled threats. They make harassing phone calls and send intimidating letters. They do just enough to let me know they know who I am and where I live. It's their not-so-subtle way of letting me know they're in control. I've never gone to the police and reported them, and they know it. They think they have me contained. That's why I'm still alive. Do you understand what I'm telling you, Mr. Lucas? I have a family to protect and a business to run."

"I fully understand, Mr. Schmidt." Dan paused and then said, "I have one request. If your nephew contacts you again, give him my number. That's all I ask."

Dan placed his business card on Schmidt's immaculate desk, but the terrorized man made no motion to take it. Instead, he stared at it as though it might turn into a rattlesnake at any moment.

"Thank you for your time, Mr. Schmidt, and, by the way, what do I owe you for today's visit?"

"Nothing. … But promise me you'll never return."

"Done."

Chapter 16
Lighting the Darkness

Dan turned the key in the brass-plated deadbolt lock and pushed the heavy wooden front door of the Radiant Love Church open while Ben stood behind him.

The large sanctuary, filled with rows of seats and a thick dark gray carpet, was eerily quiet. The air was cool, slightly musty. Waning sunlight filtered through side windows lining the expansive worship room and cast shadows throughout.

"Tim said we could have the place to ourselves tonight," Dan said as he stepped into the room. "I like the atmosphere of churches at night when they're empty and quiet."

"I can't believe I'm in a Christian church and I actually want to be here," Ben said. "What a difference a year makes. God really does come through with miracles."

"You've got that right. Glad we brought some food with us too. It's about dinnertime, and I'm getting hungry. Let's go into the fellowship hall and find us a table," Dan said.

"Good idea," Ben said. "When my blood sugar drops, I can't think. I may have a new heart and lungs, but I think God left me with the same old stomach. It doesn't like being empty for very long."

Dan and Ben laughed at the same time. They made their way through the darkened nave and into a breezeway leading to the fellowship hall where Tim's youth group met every week. They found several round tables with brown folding chairs set up. Dan chose a table in the center and placed a bag of Italian subs and bottles of water on the white plastic tabletop.

Dan distributed the foot-long hoagies when they got seated. After Ben peeled back the layers of white paper to get to his sandwich, the aroma of onions, oregano, and cold cuts wafted through the air. Dan said a short prayer thanking God for their food, and both men dug in.

"I wanted us to talk here, where we could have some real privacy," Dan said after swallowing a bite of his sandwich. "I didn't get a chance to give you the full picture of Keith's situation during our discussion in the plaza. Sorry about leaving early, but Connie distracted me with her call."

"No problem. I was reaching my saturation point anyway. I can only take so much bad news when it comes to Keith," Ben said. "As if I wasn't already dealing with enough guilt, his fate gives me outright nightmares."

"I hear you. But you know we're going to work this out, right? Your faith alone will make all the difference," Dan said.

Ben nodded. "Everything okay the other day? You looked a little upset."

Dan shrugged. "Turns out Connie's instincts were right. The publishing company that I thought was going to accept my book backed out of their conditional agreement before I even had a chance to get them my marketing plan. They must have had a staff meeting and dissected my proposal and given it a thumbs-down."

Dan paused and exhaled slowly. "I don't think I had an advocate to defend me or my manuscript. They decided I wasn't worth the risk. Now I have to figure out a way to convince them otherwise. But in the meantime, we have much more important work to do."

"I've been thinking about what you told me in the plaza," Ben said. "You know I trust your judgment, Dan, but I can't grasp how an evil group of wealthy aristocrats think they can take over the world and use my Keith to help them do it. It sounds like a wild plot from an old James Bond movie."

"The Illuminati—or whatever their true name is—was the one area of Ernie's information I doubted the most, too, so I dug in to see if I could find information that would confirm or refute what he had to say. The best way to explain it is to start at the end and work backward. I think you know me well enough to know I believe most major world events are tied in some way to what is written in the Bible. In this case, the end of the world is clearly described in the Scriptures."

Dan pulled his smartphone from his belt clip and scrolled through his apps until he found his English Standard Version digital Bible. He scanned the index and opened a book of the New Testament.

"I'm impressed," Ben said. "You've found a way to dispense with your backpack and all your notebooks and folders. I remember you pulling out your notes and Bible in the airport last year every time you wanted to make a point. You carried that pack around like it was attached to your body. Welcome to the twenty-first century."

Chuckling at Ben's good-natured dig, Dan's mind flashed back to the prior year, when he and Ben were seated on blue vinyl bench seats at the departure gate. Dan pictured Ben smirking while Dan dug through his backpack searching for a reference document to rebut a point Ben had made about the Bible being a work of fiction. Dan gave a satisfied sigh while reliving the memory and put on his glasses to read from the small screen.

"Here it is, Revelation 13. It talks about a beast who'll be present on the earth and deceive the population of the world right before the earth comes to an end in its current form. We don't know who or what the beast actually is, but some Bible scholars believe the wild beast with seven heads and ten horns introduced at Revelation 13:1 represents the worldwide political system, and they point to Revelation 13:2, which states 'it has authority, power, and a throne,' which tends to indicate it's a political entity or a ruler of one. In Revelation 13:7, it reads, and I quote, 'it rules over every tribe and people and tongue and nation,' so it's greater than a single national government. Many Christian scholars believe the beast is a person who will control the one-world government."

Ben frowned, yet kept silent.

"Regardless of who or what the beast is, the Bible clearly states that those who don't worship the beast are slain. Here it is in verses 16 and 17. 'The beast causes all, both small and great, both rich and poor, both free and slave, to be marked on the right hand or the forehead in order that no one can buy or sell unless he has the mark, that is, the name of the beast or the number of its name.' Then it goes on to say the number is 666."

"It says 666? Even I know who that stands for," Ben said.

"Yes, you do. Satan. He'll be driving the events at the end of the world as we know it. Tragically, whoever receives this mark, in whatever form it comes, will be tormented with fire and sulfur in the presence of the holy angels and in the presence of the Lamb. The Bible states that the smoke of their torment will go up forever and ever, and they'll have no rest, day or night. Ben, you personally experienced the fire in hell, so you know it exists." Dan took a moment to let his words sink in.

Ben pulled out a fresh handkerchief and rubbed it across his face. "I had no idea the Bible said that. I'm still only halfway through my Bible-in-a-year study." He swallowed hard. "Those passages are exactly right. I smelled the sulfur. Even when I was being incinerated by the greasy fire, the strong odor of sulfur burned my nasal passages like acid. People need to take this seriously! Nobody is going to want to go there if they understand what it actually is."

Ben stopped and stared at his lap for several seconds and then up at Dan. "But how? How do we make people believe? How do we get them to take the clear warnings of the Bible seriously, and how can you even explain how we could have this worldwide dictatorship that could force people to take the mark of Satan? I don't even know how that could be possible."

"We do the best we can, Ben. Like I said, you have to use facts people can verify, so they become open to the information you present them. Let's start with how you get people to take the Bible seriously and believe it's literally true. Remember when we were in Charlotte, how I laid out my case for the existence of God? I led off with the source document, the Bible. I told you it was a self-authenticating document. Remember? And how did I do that? I explained how the Bible contains sixty Messianic prophesies about the birth, life, death, and Resurrection of Jesus Christ that have already come true, and that a mathematician by the name of Dr. Peter Stoner calculated the probability of just eight of the prophecies coming true was one in ten to the seventeenth power! No book on the planet has ever had that number of specific prophesies come true. The book has a supernatural author—Father God."

"You're right," Ben said. "I remember you talking about Bible prophesies and applying probability calculations to them, but, to be frank, I wasn't ready to take your arguments seriously then. We'd barely started to have a real conversation. I need to brush up on all of the evidence you've assembled."

"I have plenty more, Ben, remember? Now to your second question: How could a worldwide dictatorship be possible? Remember Ernie the detective? His knowledge and insight opened my eyes to how it could actually happen. He's spent the last thirty years studying the process that a relatively small group of wealthy evil elite could use to create a one-world government. He believes a worldwide dictatorship is possible, and it's, in fact, being created today through a two-pronged process. One is overt and one is clandestine, to use a term from my old profession."

Ben nodded as he bit into his sandwich while keeping eye contact with Dan.

"Now consider, for a moment, Revelation 13 again. It prophesizes that either a ruler or a system of ruling will be in place to force everyone on the planet to have the same identification marking in order to buy or sell anything. The 666 marking. Total control of the world's economy couldn't happen without a true one-world government. If some leader in Europe or Asia were to emerge, for example, and try to dictate to the United States how we were to conduct our commerce, we'd laugh at him or her and ignore their order. For a dictator to be in the position to issue such an order and enforce it, there'd have to be a worldwide government already in place. As Ernie explained to me, the one-world-government advocates understand that a crucial first step in establishing a worldwide system of ruling is to create regional economic bodies that have authority over individual sovereign nations. You could accomplish such a goal by ratifying trade agreements that include mechanisms in the form of regional trade commissions that have power over all trade, labor, and commerce in a given set of countries.

"Regional trade agreements in North America, South America, Asia, Europe, and the Middle East would be needed to form the pieces that could be joined together before the beast, or anti-Christ, appears. For that to happen, nation-states would need to voluntarily relinquish their sovereignty on all economic matters. To trick people into giving up their economic freedom, say, in the United States, such agreements would have to be presented to the American people deceptively. Ernie believes that almost happened with the Trans-Pacific Partnership Agreement and could happen if the recently ratified United States-Mexico-Canada trade agreement is subverted and misapplied. The agreement establishes an independent Free Trade Commission that will govern trade over all of North America. It can change its own rules and functions, and unless the US government remains vigilant and pushes back when necessary, it could grant itself more power to control international business and commerce without the consent of US voters." Dan leaned back in the seat.

"Is that true?"

"Yes, I read key parts of the agreement myself. Now, why would our country ever want to engage in such an agreement with the potential for misuse? Because, according to Ernie, we have government officials and private citizens in positions of influence who are secretly globalists in their views, and in some cases Luciferian in their private beliefs, and they push such agreements while assuring an unsuspecting public that the agreements are a good deal. Who does he suspect is pushing these agreements from behind the scenes? Certain members of the Council on Foreign Relations, the Bilderberg Group, elements of the United Nations, the World Economic Forum, and many other groups." Dan picked up his water and took a long sip.

Ben said, "But where's the evidence for any of this? Those groups are wind factories filled with stuffy bureaucrats trying to look important."

Dan shook his head. "The groups may be filled with pretentious elitists trying to stay relevant, but what are they actually trying to accomplish? Plenty of international bodies study economics, migration patterns and the like, but what do they do secretly, in small side groups? I think the best way to evaluate the groups is to study the public pronouncements of the people of international prominence who make up the groups. As you do that, consider for a moment what a real leader committed to the security and prosperity of the United States would want to pursue. Such a person would want a free and independent America with a strong economy and a robust military. A country built on the sound foundation our forefathers created—freedom and liberty for all, based on inalienable rights from God, a timeless Constitution, the rule of law, and a republic that operates under democratic principles. You know from your academic research that many other nations are an

162

anathema to those principles. Some are outright dictatorships or quasi-authoritarian. Many are totally corrupt and some are theocracies guided by religions of death. Why would we ever want to link ourselves with those countries? How could one ruler ever be fair and equitable to all people with diverse values and beliefs? How would such a leader even be elected?"

Ben said, "How *would* such a leader be elected? You're right. That's the question."

"You know, better than most. You work at a university that teaches and promotes the very kind of thinking that leads people to seek out false leaders. Many of your fellow professors promote utopian escapism masquerading as wisdom."

Ben winced. "Ouch. I hate to admit it, but you're absolutely right."

Dan nodded and continued. "So, if you hear a group or national leader speak of the need for a new world order, you need to take a very careful look at them. We don't need a new world order run by a global dictator, we need to recognize the true world leader who already reigns in heaven, Jesus Christ. The leader who'll return to earth and establish heaven on earth after we make a complete mess of things.

"We both know the Kingdom of God is the world order we should all seek. Countries should turn to the word of God, not the deceptive and confusing bureaucratic inventions of fallen man. We are all flawed, and none of us are capable of leading the world in our current broken state. So, where do you see the evidence? Every leader who promoted or promotes a new world order, from the late Adolf Hitler to Henry Kissinger, to multiple bodies associated with the United Nations. They all deserve scrutiny."

"Kissinger? Are you serious?"

"I take him and others at their word. That's all I can do, since I didn't know him personally. No American president or cabinet official should want the United States to be part of a global world government or even a regional government that usurps American sovereignty. Look at the European Union. In thirty-six years, it went from the European Common Market, made up of six countries, to the European Union, run by unaccountable bureaucrats who make laws without the consent of the member nation-states' citizens. When you have total power, you're in a position to dictate laws that control every aspect of people's lives, including culture and religion."

"What have these people actually said?"

Dan scrolled his phone and pulled up an email. "Here, and this is one of many. This is from the late Zbigniew Brzezinski, National Security Advisor to President Jimmy Carter, and I quote, 'This regionalization is in keeping with the Trilateral Plan which calls for a gradual convergence of East and West, ultimately leading toward the goal of "one world government" …. National sovereignty is no longer a viable concept ….' Here's another one. During a World Affairs Council press conference at the Regent Beverly Wilshire Hotel on April 19, 1994, Henry Kissinger said, 'The New World cannot happen without US participation, as we are the most significant single component. Yes, there will be a New World Order, and it will force the United States to change its perceptions.'

"Bill Clinton was quoted in *USA Today*, on March 11, 1993, saying that 'We can't be so fixated on our desire to preserve the rights of ordinary Americans ….' "

Dan paused a moment, and added, "Look, I used to respect some of those people, like you do, but I totally disagree with their world views."

"I see what you mean," Ben replied while he shook his head in disbelief.

"Many other world leaders and prominent people have called for a new world order."

Dan scrolled through his emails. "Here's a small sampling of dignitaries who have publicly called for a new world order: H. G.

Wells, Bertrand Russell, Gov. Nelson Rockefeller, Pope Paul VI, Robert F. Kennedy, Richard Nixon, Fidel Castro, Mikhail Gorbachev, George Soros, Walter Cronkite, and Gen. Colin Powell. David Rockefeller even stated: 'We are on the verge of a global transformation. All we need is the right major crisis and the nations will accept the new world order.' "

Ben frowned. "Are you sure about those people?"

"I am. These are documented statements in their original context. Some world leaders have spoken openly about the threat from the globalists' influence and by inference, the Illuminati."

Dan looked back at his phone and continued to scroll. "Even the late Woodrow Wilson, a globalist himself, recognized the threat. He was quoted as saying, and here it is, verbatim, 'Some of the biggest men in the United States, in the field of commerce and manufacture, are afraid of somebody, are afraid of something. They know that there is a power somewhere so organized, so subtle, so watchful, so interlocked, so complete, so pervasive, that they had better not speak above their breath when they speak in condemnation of it.'

"President Franklin D. Roosevelt wrote, in a November 21, 1933 letter to 'Colonel' Edward Mandell House, and I quote, 'The real truth of the matter is, as you and I know, that a financial element in the large centers has owned the government of the US since the days of Andrew Jackson.' President Kennedy's father, Joseph Kennedy, wrote a letter to the *New York Times*, which appeared in the July 26, 1936 edition. In it, he stated: 'Fifty men have run America, and that's a high figure.' "

"Those men made those statements in public?"

"Yes, the letters and quotes have never been kept secret," Dan replied. "If you know where to look, you'll see the fingerprints of globalists, which were deliberately left behind."

"Like what?"

"I'll give you some recent examples. Someone changed the name of the new World Trade Center Tower from Freedom Tower to One World Trade Center. Why *that* name?"

Dan leaned forward and, not waiting for an answer, said, "How about the Denver International Airport? Unknown private donors financed the airport, which some say was totally unnecessary, and its dedication capstone reads: 'New World Airport Commission.' Who are they and why the name? The construction ran 3.8 billion dollars over budget. It included five massive buildings that were fully constructed and then declared misaligned. They were buried and never used—at least not in a publicly acknowledged way. That's not speculation—it's been corroborated. And let's not forget about the hideous end-of-world murals gracing the terminal's walls and the demon-in-a-suitcase statue. The airport even created its own website, DENfiles.com, which spoofs Illuminati theories. I explained to Tim how this is a favorite tactic to deflect scrutiny from a legitimate topic—in this case, an alleged Illuminati complex built under the guise of a new airport. Remember why Ernie thinks Klaus and Helga let Keith leave? Arrogance. Arrogance is a byproduct of evil, and arrogance is on full display at the Denver International Airport."

"But," Ben said quickly, "maybe the builders of the Denver airport and leaders like Henry Kissinger and the others you quoted have a totally different concept in mind for a new world order. Maybe they mean a world of peace, where countries act rationally and talk to each other instead of going to war. A world filled with democracies. Besides, most people would dismiss your beliefs as crazy conspiracy theories. Kissinger was a venerated diplomat and key advisor to several presidents. People would want evidence about how these great world leaders and institutions are actually linked to the occult and have concrete plans for world domination."

"You're right, Ben, and so did I. I have evidence. Let me give you a couple of examples—one hidden and one in plain sight. Have you ever heard of Lucis Trust?"

"Nope, can't say I have."

"The Lucis Trust is an entity that has many components, affiliates, and front organizations. One of its components is a publishing company that prints and disseminates the publications produced by the United Nations. A woman named Alice A. Bailey established the Lucis Trust in 1922, as Lucifer Trust. She created the Lucifer Publishing Company shortly afterward, to print and sell the books she authored. She named Lucifer Publishing Company in honor of Madame Helena Blavatsky, who cofounded the Theosophical Society. Blavatsky idolized Satan and wrote in her two-volume work, *The Secret Doctrine*, that Satan was the God of this world and the only God. I recently ran into a Russian who enlightened me as to who Blavatsky was and her work with the theosophical group.

"She greatly influenced Bailey, who claimed she was guided by the Ascended Masters. In Alice Bailey's book, *Education for a New Age*, she suggests that in the new age, 'World Citizenship should be the goal of the enlightened, with a world federation and a world brain.' In other words, a one-world government. Bailey also wrote a book, *Initiation Human and Solar*, and the title page shows the publishing house as Lucifer Publishing Co. Bailey realized the name was too truthful, so she changed it to Lucis Trust in 1923. If you go to any New Age bookstore, you'll find a lot of hard-core New Age books that are published by Lucis Trust."

"Wow, that's interesting, but how does that impact the UN today?" Ben asked.

"Lucis Trust is fully engaged with the UN as we speak, under a program called World Goodwill. It's a member of the Economic and Social Council of the United Nations."

"Are you sure?"

"Yep, and it gets better. At one point, the Lucis Trust office in New York was located at 666 United Nations Plaza. Despite its Luciferian underpinnings, many famous past and current prominent national figures have served on Lucis Trust's international board of directors. Some of the members of the board included the late Robert McNamara, former Secretary of Defense and president of the World Bank. Ditto for Thomas Watson, former IBM chairman and US Ambassador to the Soviet Union. And another name you'll recognize served on the board—Henry Kissinger."

"You've confirmed all this?"

"I have. The United Nations has long been involved in promoting a new world order and anti-Christian themes. The UN's meditation room reeks of New Age and Luciferian influences. The room was built in the shape of a truncated pyramid. The main attraction is a six-and-a-half-ton rectangular block of black magnetite polished at the top and lit from above. The stone is supposed to be an altar where the Ark of Hope is to rest. Of course, that's a complete mockery of the biblical Ark of the Covenant. Each side of the altar has symbols for earth, wind, fire, and water—symbols worshiped by modern-day pagans. There's more. A sixteen-point value system, which is a contemptuous replacement for the Ten Commandants, is also engraved on a side. The markings celebrate the virtues of a creation versus a Creator. And guess who the custodian of the meditation room is?"

"I don't know, who?"

"Lucis Trust. Some former satanic cult members allege that satanic groups have committed actual child sacrifices on the altar after hours. So, you see, there's evidence to show that the UN has been corrupted by New Ageism and covert Satanism."

"What's the evidence in plain sight?"

"The Georgia Guidestones. Some refer to them as the Illuminati's Ten Commandments or the American Stonehenge," Dan said.

"What are they and how do they help prove the Illuminati exists?" Ben asked.

"They are huge pieces of polished granite formed into a monument in Elbert County, Georgia. They stand over nineteen feet tall, are arranged with one slab standing in the center, with four larger slabs arranged around it in a uniform pattern, and a capstone that lies on top of the five slabs. The whole monument weighs around two hundred forty thousand pounds and it's astronomically aligned with the sun and the stars. A hole was drilled in the center stone to allow the North Star to be visible at any moment. Someone spent a lot of time and money creating it. It's very precise. Like a monument you'd see in Washington, DC."

"Sounds pretty harmless to me," Ben replied, "but you've obviously found some hidden nuggets that cast it in a negative light."

"What's hidden about the monument are the names of the individuals who designed and financed it. A man who called himself R. C. Christian ordered and paid for the monument in 1979, but everyone agrees the person used an alias. No one knows who he is or why he did it. What's not hidden are the messages engraved on the stones. The messages are a list of ten directives to mankind, or the Illuminati's Ten Commandments, as some researchers call them. The same ten directives are written in eight different languages— one language on each side of each stone.

"The first directive reads: 'Maintain humanity under 500,000,000 in perpetual balance with nature.' To get the world's population down to a half billion, you'd have to exterminate nine-tenths of the people alive today. Sound familiar? The third commandment is, 'Unite humanity with a living new language.' Hmm, let me see. If you have a one-world government, you'll need a one-world language to rule with. Someone or some group paid a fairly large amount of money to buy the land and pay for the monument, yet they wanted their identities secret. Wonder why?"

Ben jumped in and said, "Maybe they want to avoid publicity and get their message out without drawing attention to themselves."

"Could be," Dan replied, "but I believe the group who gave us the guidestones wants to be anonymous because they have evil plans and don't want exposure. They could be almost anyone, but they'd have to be some group or someone who could afford at least a half-million dollars."

"So, you think the person or the group is affiliated with the Illuminati and they're duty bound by some twisted code of honor or belief in karma to reveal their plans to the world?"

"Yes. You have to remember that underneath the veneer of some successful businesspeople and so-called world leaders are hearts of evil. Not all, but a select and very effective few. While they sit in their posh boardrooms, they have their criminal cartel underlings doing the dirty work. They've layered a maze of front businesses and clandestine groups between them and the individuals trafficking in children, creating child pornography, smuggling narcotics, and creating mind-controlled slaves who the elites plan to use to help take over the world.

"To achieve their goal they have to disrupt, kill, and destroy the current order. Through all of their channels, the Illuminati promote confusion, chaos, doom and gloom. Good is bad and bad is good. Confuse people about who they are, who made them, and why they're here. Tear down social institutions and create chaos so that people will gravitate toward those who promise order and stability. Who will that be? Those who rise to power secretly and who want a one-world government. All the while, people will give up their liberty for a false sense of security. Sounds nuts, but when you start to assemble the evidence, you begin to realize most of it is probably true and actually happening. We already know the Bible has told us it'll happen."

"What do we do? How do we fight them?"

"Stand strong in our faith as followers of Christ. You met Christ personally during your last NDE, something almost no one else can claim. You know he's real and that he has incredible spiritual power that emanates from Father God. Pray for his power to strengthen your faith and the faith of our fellow Americans. Christianity is the single biggest threat to the new world order. As long as we stand together and hold our ground on our faith, the global dictators will not be able to take over."

"I think I need a drink," Ben said in a serious tone. After a glance downward, he looked back at Dan with an intense expression. "For the first time in my life, I'm truly worried, but also strengthened. You lit a fire in me, Dan. You're right. It's time to take a stand, and I know where I'm gonna take mine. And you're coming with me."

Chapter 17
Coming Out

Ben stood at the base of the steps and regarded the building in which he'd spent many years. With his new knowledge and faith experiences, it appeared different to him. He straightened his shoulders. He was done hiding from truth. He knew he was among the few who realized the full cost of living the old way.

He led Dan up the broad rustic steps of the towering serpentine stone building. Large white columns framed the stately entrance of the century-and-a-half-old building. Several students exited and entered the building, most staring at phones as they shuffled along the walkway—oblivious to their surroundings.

"Aren't you taking a huge risk?" Dan asked. "You could lose your job."

"I'll lose it anyway, once word gets out," said Ben. "Liberal colleges don't tolerate stalwart professors straying from the secular reservation."

"But why during a lecture? Why not do it in a talk at the Student Union Building or someplace where you can get a voluntary audience?"

"I'd be inviting people to my own execution. I've got to do it in an environment I'm comfortable in. Besides, the element of surprise is the only way I can pull this off, and the summer session is the best time to try something risky. Fewer students means a lesser chance that someone will complain. Technically, since I'm still on sabbatical and Professor Schafer is filling in for me, I'm not officially giving a lecture as a tenured professor of this university. Maybe, by some miracle, the students will like my message and not leak it on campus. But if they do, I'm ready to face the consequences. The truth must be told. Like you said, we must take a stand."

Dan followed him through large inner double doors and into a cavernous amphitheater-shaped classroom. They arrived approximately twenty minutes before the scheduled start of class, so only a few students who had arrived early were sitting in seats and checking their phones. Ben brought Dan up to the front row and instructed him to sit to the right of the classroom's podium.

"If I get off track and get asked a question I can't answer, I'll introduce you to the class, and you can take over. Not sure how these kids will react. I have a reputation on campus of being a rabblerousing hard-ass, but since I've been on sabbatical I've become a whole lot more mellow. Funny how an encounter with Christ can change your whole outlook on life." He laughed. He wasn't even all that concerned about the consequences now that he knew his son's life was in danger.

"Your students have no idea about your NDEs?"

"Nope. I haven't told anyone on the faculty, either. All they know is that I had three coronaries—one being temporarily fatal that left me flatlined—and a miraculous recovery. A couple of my colleagues from the Science Department asked me about what happened, but I've downplayed it. I didn't want a lot of rumors to start circulating until I'd decided how I was going to handle my 'coming out' of my Christian closet and the public announcement of my NDEs."

"So, you've kept everything secret. I'm impressed. You might have survived in my old world," Dan quipped.

"Oh, I've kept my NDEs secret, but I've already begun to tweak my future lectures in small, almost imperceptible ways. Nothing flamboyant or controversial, only some minor content adjustments to get the students pointed in the direction of recognizing our great Creator. Most won't even realize what I'm doing."

The noise of a student accidentally slamming the door interrupted Ben, who glanced in the direction of several students slowly making their way into the classroom. Dan took his cue and sat down, while Ben stood at the podium and organized his notes. After the classroom was more than half full and the time reached the top of the hour, Ben cleared his throat to gain the class' attention. *It's show time, my young friends.*

"Good afternoon, everyone. For those of you who don't know me, I'm Professor Ben Chernick. I normally teach this class, but I've been on sabbatical since the middle of last year's spring semester. Professor Schafer will resume teaching this class next week."

Ben scanned the classroom and noticed he had most everyone's attention. *So far, so good.*

"Today I'm going to depart from the normal lecture and cover a topic that clearly relates to sociology. We've been learning about the development, structure, and functioning of human society. We essentially fast-forwarded from the beginning of man's existence to the state of development that required him to live in groups where the rules of interaction between fellow human beings were first established. Today I'm going to share with you an experience that will take us outside the boundaries of normal human interaction and reveal a fundamental truth about man and his essence."

Several students put down their phones and looked up simultaneously, like a herd of deer hearing an unusual sound that signaled danger.

"When we talk about the social constructions of reality, we miss an important underlying truth that impacts how man thinks, communicates, lives, and dies. Our actions are actually guided by a higher moral authority that dictates how we perceive right and wrong and how those perceptions influence our interactions with others."

Ben took a few seconds to observe the students. "What am I talking about? Every human being has a spirit and soul that contains our fundamental nature as a person—our thoughts, our senses, our memories, and our beliefs—our personalities. Our personalities are what allow us to interact with other human beings. I'm not talking about the molecules and neurons and synapses that make up our brains. I'm talking about a construct in another space-time continuum that we can't see, touch, or analyze. It's a construct that's real and infinitely more complex than our brains. It's a construct that guides the very essence of our social interactions and our social norms as human beings."

Ben stepped away from the podium and slowly paced back and forth in front of the classroom. He was in his element and knew his topic. *It feels good to be back.*

"How do I know this? I transitioned from the use of my physical brain to my spirit-soul mind three times last year. I died, physically. My heart stopped three times, and after the third time, I was pronounced dead by an attending physician. I have an eyewitness with me today who was present during two of the times my heart stopped beating."

A collective gasp consumed the room. Ben smiled and scanned the young faces of his captive audience. *Got 'em.*

"Didn't see that one coming, did you? Well, your young minds need to grasp what I'm about to tell you. This may be the only time in your life you'll hear it. There is more to life than matter and energy as we know it. Some of you may be aware that I was on sabbatical most of last year. What you probably don't know is that while I was dead—physically—for fourteen minutes in a hospital bed in Charlotte, North Carolina, my mind, my very essence as a person, never died. My mind was fully intact. In fact, during those three heart attacks, I left my body each time and traveled to another location that is not on any map. A location that has a name familiar to every person in this room." He paused again to let his words sink in and so they'd listen to the next four he was going to say.

"That location was hell."

The classroom erupted into a growing din of loud murmurs. Dan turned in his seat to watch the students, who were shifting in their seats and staring at each other. Some muttered to their neighbors. Some seemed agitated. Ben gave him a look of concern. Dan nodded, as if to confirm Ben was on the right track.

Without raising his voice, Ben continued. "I know what I'm saying may be hard to believe. I know if someone had told me this before my experiences, I would have rejected it. … But it did happen, and not sharing it with you would be morally wrong. You have a right to know the realities of your existence, even if you're not taught about it in any other classroom on this campus or at home. I thought this physical world was all there is, but I was wrong. We do have a consciousness that resides outside our bodies, and it is far more capable than our brains."

A student raised his hand. "Professor, what was hell like?"

Several students laughed.

Ben grinned and thought how different he'd have reacted a year ago. "I know it sounds bizarre. I was an atheist before my experiences and didn't believe in heaven or hell, but I can tell you now they are real. I know—I'm an eyewitness. And let's not forget that we also learn of the existence of these phenomena, these otherworldly destinations, through organized religion, which is a social institution. At the heart of most organized religions is a source document. A collection of writings—writings that give man insights into who we are, how we were made, and what we will do when we take our last breath.

"Books, stories, journals and the like are all, in a sense, social constructs used for communicating cultural and social norms and information. But some documents fulfill a much greater purpose. Some describe the secrets of life and death. I was an eyewitness to the truths about death that are clearly explained in one document—and one document only—the Bible."

"Eyewitness to what truths?" a student asked.

"Jesus Christ is a real, living, supernatural being. He rescued me the third time I went to hell."

Ben lost complete control of the class. Several students shouted over the din, and several got up and left the classroom. Ben shot another frantic glance toward Dan, who again nodded to assure him he was on track.

"All right, all right," shouted Ben. *Why did I think this was a good idea?*

"Professor, none of what you said has been proven. Why should we believe you?" a student asked when the others had settled down.

"Because I'm standing here telling you it did. I was clinically dead for fourteen minutes, and here I am with absolutely no adverse effects. I should have never self-resuscitated. No one is dead for fourteen minutes and comes back to life on their own, but I did, and I have the medical records to prove it. I have no brain damage. No cognitive impairment of any kind."

The class erupted in laughter.

Ben chortled and shook his head. "I set myself up for that one, didn't I? I'm not surprised you feel this way. But if you don't want to believe me, here's my colleague, Mr. Dan Lucas, who's a retired NCIS special agent and an expert on near-death experiences, which is what I had, and he'll give you some factual background on the subject."

Surprised by Ben's sudden announcement, Dan stood and faced the class.

The students stopped talking and eyed the unexpected guest speaker.

"Now, I know some of you are skeptical about the professor's story. Yes, it sounds unbelievable, but it's a lot more common than you might think. A poll by Pew Research showed that about five percent of the respondents experienced a near-death experience, or an NDE, as they're called. That means millions of people around the world have experienced an NDE."

The undercurrent of chatter and whispers stopped.

"Your professor mentioned that his experiences confirmed what is written in the Bible. I can tell you from firsthand experience that the professor is not motivated by religious convictions to fabricate a story. I was with Professor Chernick the night he had two of his three heart attacks in the Charlotte Douglas International Airport. I watched him collapse and lapse into semiconsciousness both times."

The class became dead silent.

"When our night together began, we were complete strangers. An ice storm caused all flights to be canceled and all roads in the area of the airport to be closed, leaving us stranded in the terminal for more than twelve hours. Professor Chernick and I ended up seated next to each other in the terminal, and I can tell you the professor was anything but a religious man or a follower of Christ."

Dan scanned the class.

"I'm a follower of Christ, and I spent nearly twelve hours trying to convince him, through evidence, that the Bible is true. He rejected everything I had to say, but now, here he is, confirming what I knew to be true. We do live on after clinical death and we do have a Creator who lives in a supernatural world that none of us can fathom. How do I know this? Not only from reading the Bible, but by studying the research of countless doctors and scientists who have documented that man's consciousness exists external to his body. Many people have shared eyewitness accounts that were very similar to the professor's."

The students remained silent and focused on Dan as he talked. Ben relaxed and let out a breath he didn't realize he was holding. He was almost as mesmerized by Dan as the class was.

"You're all very lucky. You have an educated man who can tell you firsthand what he experienced. You can reject or accept it—the choice is yours. But I suggest you listen carefully to what the professor has to say, and keep an open mind. I spent thirty years of my life collecting, analyzing, and preserving evidence. I know real evidence when I see it, and your professor has evidence, eyewitness testimony, that can change your life."

Ben went back to the podium. All the students watched the two speakers.

"Thank you, Dan. For those of you who are interested in the details, you can stay after class. For the rest of you, Professor Schafer will be covering chapters three and four for the next class."

Ben wasn't sure they'd reached a single student, but they'd tried. More importantly, *he'd* tried. Still, he was sure his resignation showed on his face. He'd probably ended his career and hadn't made any difference.

He knew it wouldn't be long before he found out how bad it could be.

***

The Flagler Hospital nurse in the gold-and-violet teddy bear scrubs adjusted the IV drip line connected to a clear plastic bag filled with an antibiotic. She occasionally glanced at the small child huddled in the middle of the hospital bed under a pile of white blankets. The diffused light from the fluorescent fixture over the bed reflected softly off the young girl's nearly hairless head. The repeated bouts of chemo had stripped her of her beautiful blond hair and emaciated her frame. The little one tried to force a weak grin as she watched the nurse.

"Is there anything else you need, Julie?" the pretty Filipino nurse asked while making notations on the room's computer terminal connected to the wall by a movable support arm. "How about something to drink?"

"No, thank you," the young child said before lapsing into a coughing spasm.

Liz Williams, seated in a nearby chair, looked up from her paperback and went over to rearrange Julie's blanket and feel her forehead for signs of a fever.

"Maybe later," Liz said. "She finished a cup of juice before you came in. If her dad were here, he'd be making sure she kept drinking fluids. He was big on staying hydrated." Liz realized she had been thinking out loud and that the nurse wouldn't understand what she was talking about.

"I haven't seen your daddy yet," the nurse said in the direction of Julie, "but I'm sure he'll want you to drink your juice."

"Oh, he's in heaven," Julie announced in a weak, matter-of-fact tone.

The nurse realized she had innocently blundered. "Oh, I'm so sorry," she said, sending a pleading expression in Liz's direction.

"That's okay," Liz said in a resigned tone. "Her daddy's been gone now for over a year. We all miss him, but we know he's watching over us."

The nurse tried to appear cheerful as she winced mentally.

"Julie, do you want to watch some cartoons?" Liz asked.

The child shook her head and closed her eyes.

Tim entered the room as the nurse was leaving. *Time to bring some positive energy to our little girl.*

"Hi, Uncle Tim," Julie said in a barely audible voice.

She appeared to have sensed his arrival while her eyes were still closed. She peeked at him and forced a weak smile.

"How's my girl doing?" He sat in a chair next to Liz and kept his gaze on Julie.

She opened her eyes and repositioned to face him. "I'm fine, Uncle Tim."

"Now, that's what I like to hear," he said with a wink.

Liz gave him a worried glance and shifted her gaze back at Julie. "The antibiotics have brought down her fever, but she's still congested and has a bad cough. The doctors want to transfer her to

Wolfson and do a stem cell transplant as soon as they clear up the pneumonia."

Liz tried to appear confident as she spoke, but Tim could sense her stress.

Why, Lord? Please help us all and heal this little girl. He gently patted her on the shoulder.

"Julie, I want to pray for you now. Is that okay?"

Julie nodded briskly, pulled a small teddy bear close to her, and closed her eyes.

***

Ben checked his watch as several students left the classroom. *Probably headed to their next class.*

A surprising number stayed behind. From the lectern, he glanced at Dan and shrugged. Dan gave him a thumbs-up and sat in the closest seat.

"All right, I see we have quite a few of you who want to hear more."

More than a dozen hands shot up.

"Okay, I'll try to get to all of you." Pointing to a young man wearing an orange T-shirt and faded jeans, Ben said, "Go ahead."

"Professor, how do you know you had a real experience and didn't hallucinate while you were having your heart attacks?"

"Hallucinations are filled with random, often disjointed thoughts and visual images that fade with time. They usually have no clear beginning, end, or a logical progression of experiences. They also normally don't fit an established pattern that has been identified through peer-reviewed research studies, as has been the case with NDEs. My experiences were so vivid that I can recall even minute details today. I also suffer from symptoms of minor post-traumatic stress syndrome. Even today, when I recall the events, my blood pressure goes up. No dream or hallucination can have that kind of effect on a person over the long term."

"Professor, what is hell like?"

"Hell's not only a place, but it's another world that defies description. I can't accurately capture the essence of hell with mere words. During each of my NDEs, I went to different parts of hell. As our earth has mountains and valleys and lakes and oceans, hell has many different features too. My first NDE took me to a place of almost complete darkness that had a living, physical quality to it. My second NDE took me to a large cavernous area, probably many miles wide, lined with shallow pits on the cavern's floor that had flame jets at the bottom. My last NDE took me to an area that had cells made of stone and bars and doors made of a metallic substance. The cell area was connected to a much larger cavern that had a huge lake of thick flaming liquid. Every location had incredible heat, hardly any air to breathe, nauseating smells, and deafening screams and noises."

"Did you feel pain while you were in hell?"

"Yes, I did—excruciating agony—and anyone who claims otherwise is either ignorant or lying. One of the many lies told about hell is that it's merely a place where we're separated from God, sort of an eternal time out. More importantly, for reasons we don't have time to address today, there's a concerted effort from a number of fronts, to persuade people that hell doesn't exist—that all people go to heaven. If you happen to be an agnostic or an atheist, like I used to be, you believe the lie that when you die, physically, your mind stops functioning and you cease to exist while your body slowly decomposes. Absolute rubbish. Not only does your consciousness exist in the form of your soul, but your body is replicated by your spirit in a supernatural time-space continuum where your senses are heightened, your ability to think and recall are greatly enhanced, and you can sense pain, thirst, hunger, and crushing fear. I felt constant agonizing pain that would have caused a human on earth to go into shock and collapse into unconsciousness."

A hush settled over the students.

Okay, maybe this won't be a complete waste of time, after all.

"Remember, I'm talking about reality here, not religion. We do have a Creator who has blessed us with the gift of life. All he asks in return is love and respect. He doesn't care about your religious affiliation or your lack of religious knowledge. He only cares that you truly believe he exists, you have faith in him, and you try to obey his laws. Most of all, just as he loves you, he asks you to truly love him as your Creator—a supernatural parent for eternity."

When another student raised her hand, a fellow professor strode into the room to teach the next class.

"We've run out of time for today," Ben said. "For those of you who'd like to continue the discussion, come to my office."

In the hallway, Ben gave Dan a worried look. "Did I seal my fate?"

"You sealed the fate of some of your students for eternity. You planted the seeds. Some will grow."

There's no going back now, Ben thought. *And frankly, I'm glad.*

Chapter 18
Breaking the News

Dan Lucas kept pace as Ben Chernick marched briskly past a block of aging row houses and crossed W. Girard Avenue, onto N. Third Street in North Central Philadelphia. Dan's head swiveled, constantly scanning the streets and sidewalks of the mid-1900s neighborhood, on guard for threats. Ben checked the google map app on his phone as he guided Dan through the somewhat deserted mixed-use area of commercial and multiunit residential buildings several miles from Temple University's main campus. Cars in need of a good washing lined both sides of the one-way street. Several trees in full bloom provided sporadic shade in the concrete, asphalt, and brick habitat.

Ben stopped in front of a two-story, reddish-brown brick building that resembled a refurbished factory. The bronze window and door frames of the converted condo complex gave the building a solid and upscale appearance.

"This is it," Ben said. "It looks fairly new. Good to see Nicole's living in a decent place. I was worried when she told me her condo was in North Philly, but this is pretty nice. She must be doing well to afford a place here."

Ben approached the main entrance. Near the single large glass door, a covered keypad and intercom headset were mounted on the left side. He lifted the hinged Plexiglas cover and punched in Nicole's condo number; he listened to the ringtone on the headset.

A soft female voice answered, "Hello."

"Nicole, it's Ben. I'm here with Dan."

A loud buzzing sound was followed by an audible click. Ben pulled open the door and escorted Dan in.

"Follow me."

The two made their way along an inner hallway of off-white walls and a floor of large grayish-white tiles. At Nicole's condo entrance Ben pressed the doorbell, and within a few seconds Nicole opened the door.

Dressed in a short-sleeved rust-colored blouse and trim-fitting jeans, she paused for a second before giving Ben a reluctant hug. She forced a smile that creased the few lines on her face, which was covered with a fresh application of makeup. In her late thirties, Nicole retained a youthful appearance, although the ravages of stress were starting to appear in the form of furrows on her forehead.

"Nicole, this is my good friend Dan Lucas I told you about. He's been an incredible help."

"Hello, Dan." Nicole shook Dan's hand and welcomed them into her home. She scrutinized Dan from head to toe and then turned to Ben.

"You have a beautiful home," Ben said. "You'd never guess these places were so big, from the outside." Ben quickly assessed the two-thousand-square-foot condo, the vaulted ceiling, and second-story loft. The space had luxurious hardwood floors and contemporary furniture. "This is a huge place for a single woman."

Nicole nodded with a confirming look of satisfaction. "I bought it after the crash of '08. I was in the right place at the right time. They had finished the building right after the market tanked and wanted to unload the units. Maybe I'll be able to fill it now, if Keith decides he wants to stay here. You do know where he is, correct? That's why you wanted to see me, right?"

Ben cleared his throat and shot a nervous glance at Dan.

With his focus on Nicole, Ben said, "We came here to give you the full picture of what Dan has found. Like I told you on the phone,

Dan's a retired NCIS agent with years of investigative experience. He's done a lot of complex national security cases, and this one took all of his skills."

Nicole narrowed her eyes and stared at Ben and then Dan.

Ben said, "It's complicated and difficult to explain over the phone. That's why I was vague. I didn't want to worry you. I knew you'd have questions. Dan suggested we come here so we could take our time and talk."

"So, what are you saying? I thought you tracked him down."

"Not exactly," Dan said. "We know a lot about his foster parents and his probable upbringing, and why he likely left home, but we don't know where he is yet."

"What?" Nicole was visibly upset. She dropped into an overstuffed white leather armchair and glared at Ben.

Ben and Dan sat on opposite ends of a larger leather sofa that faced Nicole.

"But you said you had leads on Keith's whereabouts."

"I didn't want to get you worried and not be able to answer all your questions," Ben said. "Dan was gracious enough to travel to Portland to try and get some answers about Keith. Dan never approached your uncle Klaus or aunt Helga, but he did come back with a lot of information. That's why we're here. Dan needs to explain what he found and what it means for Keith. Go ahead, Dan."

"Nicole, I'm not sure what you know about your aunt and uncle, but I believe you've probably suspected something was different about them."

"I did. My family was not close. My parents never visited Uncle Klaus or Aunt Helga, and they never visited us. My father seemed to tolerate Klaus. I never once saw my father smile when Klaus' name came up, and when they talked on the phone, my father always seemed stressed. Uncle Klaus was very interested in my younger brother Michael, but my father always kept Uncle Klaus away from him."

"How about when you lived with your aunt and uncle, when you gave birth to Keith?"

"I've sort of blocked a lot of it out of my memory. I do remember they have a large home. I stayed in the guest wing. I also remember they had a basement that was always locked. I was under so much stress with the pregnancy that I mostly stayed in my room until I delivered Keith. Once he was born, Klaus and Helga became impatient with me. I sensed they wanted me to leave right after the baby was born. They hired a nanny who was to take care of him. She would take him for long periods every day, until he needed to be fed. About a week after I gave birth to Keith, a woman they addressed as Grandmother came to the house to see Keith. I wasn't in the room when the nanny showed Keith to her, but I heard Klaus address the woman in a way that made me think she was not a real grandmother or family relative, but someone in a position of great authority. The woman only came to the house once when I was there. Everything else was pretty much a blur from then on. After I left Portland, I moved in with my sister here in Philly, and later I went back to school and finished my graduate work and got a teaching position. The first couple of years were hard. I kept thinking about Keith and blamed myself for not keeping my child. Despite how I felt, I honored my pledge to let Uncle Klaus and Aunt Helga raise Keith, though. I thought it would be in his best interests."

Dan then commenced the delicate task of explaining to Nicole the reality of who and what her aunt and uncle were. After hearing the full picture of Klaus and Helga's involvement in the Illuminati, Nicole sobbed uncontrollably for several minutes. Ben comforted her and attempted to lift her spirits.

"Look, you did what you thought was best for our son. I understand how you feel now, but you can't blame yourself. I'm the cause of this mess, so it's up to me to right this wrong. We'll find him."

"We have to find him," Nicole said. "He can stay here when you do. I feel so guilty that I didn't take care of him."

"Not as guilty as I feel, but the past is the past, and our emotions won't help Keith now."

"You're right," Dan said. "We have to stay on point and do everything we can to locate him while he's on the run. His life may depend on it."

***

The middle-aged man in the medium gray summer-weight suit took off his reading glasses and stared across his large walnut desk at Ben Chernick, who was seated in an armchair in front of the desk, like a student who had been summoned to the principal's office.

"Ben, we've received complaints from some of the students in one of your Intro to Sociology courses. They claim you taught a class last week. Aren't you still on sabbatical?"

"I am, but I asked Professor Schafer to let me sub for him for one class, to let me try out some new lecture material."

"The students who complained believe you've converted your class into a seminar on religion."

Ben sat motionless in front of the dean of the Department of Social Sciences, and said, "Ted, I didn't convert my class into a religious seminar. I shared a personal experience with them that ties in to our subject matter. I wanted to open their eyes and minds to the reality of the world around us and the universe we inhabit. Isn't that what we're supposed to do in a university? Expose students to new ideas?"

"Not when those ideas form an argument for believing in the Bible. We have a religious studies program, and that's not your lane in the road. Ben, you've had a great teaching career with this fine institution. Don't spoil it with this come-to-Jesus phase that you're apparently in."

Ted glanced down at his executive desk covered with strategically placed mementos while collecting his thoughts. "I must say you went through quite a lot with your heart attacks. Maybe we should extend your sabbatical. Give you some more time to sort out your personal life and get your focus back on teaching."

"Ted, we've known each other for a long time. You know what I teach and how I teach it. I'd never add any content to my courses if I didn't think it was essential. At the very heart of man's interaction with his fellow man is his inner self. His thoughts and emotions. Many of those thoughts are formed through interactions with other human beings, but some come from a supernatural source we've never fathomed. A source that I experienced. These kids need to know that the bonds they develop with people are the result of more than mere molecules and flesh-and-blood interactions. There's a component in each of us, our soul, which determines who we are, how we think, and what we do. Our soul was designed by our Creator. To ignore the most important component of our makeup as human beings would be educational malpractice. I know it's new and not clearly understood, but we have to start somewhere. We have to begin to explore it, and my very brief introduction of the subject in my class will serve to only expand the minds of the students and prompt them to learn more."

"Ben, you know we have boundaries we have to respect as an institution. What you said in class bothered some of the students, and, apparently, you had a federal law enforcement officer with you who's an expert in the phenomenon you experienced. Is that true?"

"Yes, his name is Dan Lucas. He's a retired NCIS special agent who's a writer and has done quite a bit of research into near-death experiences. That's what I had, Ted, a near-death experience. I experienced a whole new dimension that we pass into when our bodies stop functioning. I want to bring what I learned into the classroom to educate, not indoctrinate. The students won't be tested on the material. I added it to enrich their educational experience and expand their intellectual horizons. I make no apologies for adding worthwhile material to my class."

"I have to answer the complaints and give a report to the provost, so I need you to give me something in writing to make this go away."

"You don't have to worry about this semester, Ted. I've made my presentation and will turn the class back over to Professor Schafer. I'll update my course content when I return in the fall, but I can't say I won't include some of it if I feel it enhances our class discussions."

"I can say for sure you *won't* include it next year, Ben. That's not a request, that's an order. Understood?"

Ben exhaled deeply and stared at the floor. He got the response he knew he'd get.

"Loud and clear." Ben stood and walked out. The die had been cast.

***

Dan Lucas parked his freshly detailed Dodge Charger in the associate pastor's reserved parking space and headed toward the Radiant Love Church building's side entrance. Dan was beginning to feel familiar with the church's layout. He found Tim Williams in his office, with the door open. Tim was on the phone, and when he saw Dan, he nodded and ended the call.

"Thanks for driving down, Dan. Please, have a seat. I've been thinking more about what you told me about Genesis 6 and did some reading on my own. You were right. Not many pastors talk about it, but there are a fair number of respected Bible scholars I discovered who interpret the passages the way that you do, and I must say, the plain language meaning of the words is hard to ignore. The only area of real disagreement I saw was how the Nephilim reappeared on the earth after the Great Flood."

"Tim, I don't think you need to go into a lot of detail with an exploration of Genesis 6 in your Sunday messages. Maybe a sermon on its basic content and an occasional reminder of its importance in later sermons, when you can make a tie-in. Your congregation needs to know that our God is not a bloodthirsty killer who wipes out people indiscriminately. They need to understand that God is holy and acts in ways we can't comprehend, but he's not evil. Evil comes from Satan and his invisible dark kingdom."

"I understand, but it's difficult for people to make fine distinctions and connect the past to the present. We see evil in the world every day, but we attribute it to man being fallen. I'm trying to make a connection with how giants in the past have any link with what's going on in the world today," Tim said.

"You're on the right track. Yes, the events of Genesis 6 took place thousands of years ago, but there are events happening today that could be directly linked to the fallen angels."

Tim straightened in his chair and leaned forward. "How so? I know you told me some folks found skeletons of giants years ago, and when they were found, they mysteriously disappeared after being confiscated by authorities. I also remember the newspaper articles you showed me from decades ago that documented the findings of huge skeletons, but old news doesn't have much impact on people today."

"Tim, the most important message for pastors to deliver is not what happened to the bones of the Nephilim. The message for the masses is to get them to start considering whether there is a real likelihood of a connection between the fallen angels who fathered the Nephilim and some current events of today."

Dan paused and glanced down for a few moments, collecting his thoughts. "Let me ask you something. If you were a prison warden, what would be one of your top concerns?"

"Oh, I don't know. Probably worrying about the most dangerous criminals making an escape."

"And why worry about the criminals making an escape, other than the obvious concern about losing your job?"

"They might kill people if they were murderers."

"Exactly!"

Tim looked confused. "I'm not following you."

"You've described precisely what the Bible warns about in veiled terms. In 2 Peter, second chapter, verse 4, the Bible documents how God punished some of the fallen angels—the sons of God we talked about—by casting them into a specific place called Tartarus, a place deep inside the earth that is a literal physical prison. They're still there waiting to be freed. If they get loose, they'll have vengeance on their minds. And there may be others in the dark abode who are also waiting for the right time to reappear."

"Wow, you're getting far afield, Dan. Sounds like something Hollywood would dream up."

"I know it sounds wild, but you believe the Bible, don't you?"

"Of course I do, but I still don't see the connection with any of this and the present day."

"What if I told you there may be a current effort that could accidentally free those imprisoned fallen angels and potentially release them back into our environment, where they could wreak havoc? What if I told you the same effort might also bring other evil spiritual entities into our physical dimension?"

"I'd say you've watched too many horror movies. With all due respect, that sounds crazy."

"Have you ever heard the term CERN?"

"The name sounds familiar, but I don't remember any more."

"Most people don't. It's the acronym for the European Organization for Nuclear Research, a scientific exploratory organization that operates the largest particle physics laboratory in the world. It's located in Switzerland, and part of the facility is in France."

"Okay, I do remember hearing about it, but I don't know anything about it."

"All right. The main feature of the facility is the Large Hadron Collider, a very powerful machine that smashes subatomic particles together at incredible speeds. The scientists record the collisions and study the byproducts to learn more about matter and its origins."

Tim squinted and stared at Dan. "Dan, I respect you and all, and I know you've done a lot of research, but to be honest, I don't see the significance of any of what you're talking about. You've described a scientific research facility that I'm sure fascinates the science professors and those who study physics and such, but as far as the congregation in my church making a connection between CERN, and giants, and fallen angels, and havoc in the world, I don't see it."

"Great segue, Tim. You just explained why most of the planet doesn't pay any attention to CERN. But for those of us who do, there's enough circumstantial evidence to make us stop and think."

"What circumstantial evidence? What in the world are you talking about?" Tim's faced reddened. He stopped when he realized he was raising his voice.

"All right, here goes." Dan reached into his briefcase and pulled out one of his blue folders brimming with research materials.

"One of the stated goals of CERN was to locate the subatomic particle, the Higgs boson, which many have dubbed 'the God particle.' It accomplished that goal on the 4th of July, 2012. Others have described the function of CERN as re-creating the process of creation itself or replicating the conditions immediately after the so-called Big Bang. So here we have researchers saying their goal is to reach into the domain of God and his creation, and figure it out independent of God. Now, some would disagree with my characterization, but I think it fits. You can do the research and find the same statements. The scientists are not trying to hide them."

"Okay," Tim said. "I agree that's interesting from a theological perspective, but I hope there's more."

"There's a lot more. One of the goals of CERN is to determine why there is more matter than antimatter in the universe. Some believe the CERN experiments conducted to answer such questions could make a higher dimensional black hole or a hole in our time-space continuum. Could something come through one of those holes?"

"You're talking about a highly theoretical possibility of something going wrong during a scientific experiment," Tim said. "I can't sell that to the church as proof of some supersmart scientists doing the work of the devil. You have no proof."

"Right again, Tim. If you focus only on the scientific aspects of CERN, you'll miss what may be actually going on."

Dan fished through his notes, pulled out a printed page, and skimmed the document. "Consider this for a minute and tell me what you think. In the center of the CERN facility is a large statue of the Hindu god, Shiva. Shiva is known as the god of destruction, or the transformer within the Trinity. Why have a mythological symbol of a destroyer as the centerpiece for your corporate headquarters? Also, the logo for CERN has what appears to be three numeral sixes arranged around the letters *C E R N*. The sign of Satan, 666. A coincidence? Maybe. Others say the logo was inspired by the design of devices known as synchrotron particle accelerators. Not sure which is true, but the result happens to look like three sixes."

Tim sat quietly and listened.

"It gets better." Dan pulled some additional sheets from the blue folder and traced some lines with his right index finger as he read to himself. Then he said, "Here's something for a sermon you could use to get your congregation's attention. CERN's Large Hadron Collider is partially situated in a town in France called Saint-Genis-Pouilly. The name "Pouilly" comes from the Latin, *Appolliacum*. Researchers have determined that CERN is located dead center over the remains of an ancient Roman temple built for the god Apollo, also known as Abaddon. The site is also known as the gateway to the underworld, or the top of the bottomless pit. Here's the Bible verse that's directly germane. Revelation 9, verses 1 and 2: 'And the fifth angel blew his trumpet, and I saw a star fallen from heaven to earth, and he was given the key to the shaft of the bottomless pit. He opened the shaft of the bottomless pit, and from the shaft rose smoke like smoke of a great furnace, and the sun and the air were darkened with the smoke from the shaft.' Verse 11: 'They have as king over them the angel of the bottomless pit. His name in Hebrew is Abaddon and in Greek he is Apollyon.' What a coincidence, right!"

"Dan, I can see how people could say CERN is up to no good, and I know all of the symbolism makes you wonder, but can't people just say it's a respected research facility studying advanced science?"

"Let's let the former director of CERN answer your question for me."

Dan paused for a minute as he read through his notes. "Here it is. CERN's very own former director-general and its director of research, General Rolf Heuer, told the press that one of the goals of CERN's Large Hadron Collider was to open a portal to another dimension. In his own words, he said, 'When we open the door, something might come through it into our reality! Or, we might send something through it into their reality!' Even without identifying what might use that portal, it's a pretty alarming event, right?"

"Wow. Why aren't the Bible scholars talking about this?" Tim said.

"Some are, but they get no publicity, and the media shuns this type of information. What's interesting is that even atheists have sounded the alarm about CERN. The late Stephen Hawking said the result of CERN's research could pose grave dangers to our planet. In his words, 'the God Particle, the Higgs boson found by CERN, could destroy the universe.' Neil deGrasse Tyson, another atheist and also a physicist and director of the Hayden Planetarium, also believes, like Hawking, that the experiments being planned and conducted at CERN are a legitimate danger to the future of mankind."

"Why doesn't somebody do something about it?"

"No one knows what's truly going on and no single government has the power to stop them. They do as they please. Right now, they're trying to re-create the conditions of the so-called Big Bang. To do that, they've worked hard to double the power output of the Large Hadron Collider. It's the biggest machine in the world, and it has magnets that are one hundred thousand times more powerful than the gravitational pull of Earth. Some of the experiments are believed to be capable of generating temperatures more than one hundred thousand times the temperature at the center of the sun. It all gets back to CERN's institutional belief in the existence of other parallel and alternate dimensions, and their belief that in increasing the LHC's power output and in re-creating the conditions of the Big Bang, CERN scientists can rip open the veil that separates our dimension from others, and that would expose us to what's in the other dimensions."

"So, we're essentially helpless. I don't know what good a sermon about it would do," Tim said.

"It would make your congregation think. And when enough people start to get concerned about a problem, they take action. The worst thing we could do right now would be to stay silent and ignore the problem. Knowledge is power. Gain as much as you can and then share it."

"I guess you're right. But to be honest, Dan, you'd be a better candidate to deliver a message on CERN during a sermon, than I would. You know the details and can tie it to Scripture. Why don't you speak at one of our services? You could also talk about your book. We talked about this before. What do you say?"

"I guess you're right. I'm good at finding ways for other people to engage evil and speak the truth, but I shy away from doing the heavy lifting myself. Time for me to get my act together. Let me start to put something together and I'll get back to you."

When Dan stopped speaking, he paused and stared out the window. *No more sitting on the sidelines. Time to put up or shut up.*

Chapter 19
Push Comes to Shove

"I'll be right with you, sir."

Keith Schmidt slid the glass take-out window shut and turned back to the stainless-steel drink dispenser to finish filling the last large paper cup with ice and Coke Zero. He pressed the tight-fitting plastic lid down on the waxed cup's lip and glanced at the computer screen to check the list of food and drinks for order #52.

He placed three Big Barn Special Burgers, three large drinks, and three large fries securely in the gray paper take-out tray. Satisfied the order was complete and ready to go, he returned to the take-out window and handed the top-heavy paper tray of food and drinks to the bearded thirty-something man waiting in an idling F-150 pickup.

"There you go, sir. I put in some extra catsup packets for you. Thank you for choosing Burger Barn."

Keith slid the glass closed as the deep pulsating exhaust sounds from the accelerating truck resonated under the window's awning. He turned to find a team member, Susan, standing behind him. Her medium brown hair, pulled into a ponytail, gleamed under the fast-food restaurant's fluorescent lights. At five feet five, she seemed small next to Keith's lanky six-foot frame. She had stepped away from the cash register after the last customer in line had paid.

"I thought it was time for you to go on break," she said with a smile. "I can take over for you if you want to go sit down. Monica is back on the register now."

"Okay, thanks. I guess I lost track of the time. I like keeping busy. Not much else to do and no place to go."

Susan tilted her head and studied his face for several seconds. Her round hazel eyes were framed with tastefully applied eyeliner.

"What do you mean, you have no place to go? You do have a home, don't you?"

Keith looked at the floor—embarrassed to tell Susan the truth. *What a loser she'll think I am.* "Ah, not right now. I moved out of my apartment a while back and have been sleeping in my car. I didn't feel safe where I was living and haven't found a new place yet."

"Ah, okay, I understand. ... If you're looking for something to do, my church group is having a cookout at the beach pavilion on Saturday. You're welcome to join us. You don't need to bring anything, just yourself. I can ask my friends if they know of any good apartments for rent, too."

Keith visibly stiffened. "I'm not much into church stuff." His stomach tightened and he felt the urge to flee. A voice whispered in his head, *Stay away.*

"Don't worry, no burgers and fries. We're gonna grill some chicken and ribs. Besides, we're a pretty harmless group. Our pastor will be there and he might be able to help you with a place to stay until you find a place of your own. No pressure. Let me know if you change your mind. We like sharing the Good News with people and having a good time."

"The Good News?"

"Yeah, you know. Jesus loves us all. I can't think of any news better than that. You can come and see it for yourself. You'll see why we follow the road he's leading us on."

When the words "follow the road" penetrated Keith's psyche, he began to sway back and forth while his eyes darted side to side rapidly. He then collapsed forward, directly into Susan's arms. The weight of his body pushed her momentarily back into the wall until she was able to step one foot back to brace herself and prevent him from falling. She regained her balance and was able to help Keith stand upright.

"Keith, Keith, what's wrong. Are you all right?"

He went limp, and then his arms and body violently jerked uncontrollably. The shift supervisor standing near the grills ran over and helped Susan ease Keith down into a sitting position on the floor. The other restaurant workers came over to see what was happening. Keith moaned and continued shaking.

"Keith, Keith," the shift supervisor said.

No response. Keith continued to shake and bob his head.

Susan glanced up at the supervisor. "Do you want me to call 911?"

"Let's see what's wrong with him. Keith, can you hear me?" the supervisor asked.

Keith blinked rapidly and stopped twitching. "Yeah," Keith said in a whisper.

"I think you need to go to the hospital. Can you stand up?" Susan asked.

"Yeah, I think so." Keith's speech was slow and weak. He felt horrible.

Susan and the shift supervisor slowly helped Keith back to his feet and steadied him while they looked into his eyes. The movement of his eyes back and forth slowed gradually.

"Do you want me to drive him to the ER?" Susan asked. "Might be better than having an ambulance come here. Wouldn't be too good for business, don't you think?"

"Yeah, good idea," the shift supervisor said. "We're slow now, anyway, and I can call in some relief if we get busy again. Do you want to use your car or mine?"

"Mine. I have my dad's SUV. It has a big front seat."

Susan and the shift supervisor slowly guided Keith through the nearly empty parking lot, toward the maroon Chevy Traverse. While they helped him get into the passenger side, he kept blinking. Using his own power, he positioned himself in the seat and leaned his head back against the headrest before closing his eyes. Pain gripped his head like a vise. His mind went blank.

"Hold on. We'll be at the hospital in a few minutes," he heard Susan say from a thousand miles away.

She eased out into St. Augustine traffic and made the short drive to the hospital while keeping an eye on Keith. Within ten minutes of negotiating early afternoon traffic, she pulled into the closest parking space near Flagler Hospital's emergency room entrance and helped Keith out as he was starting to regain his composure.

Holding him by his left arm and shoulder, she slowly guided him under the large red EMERGENCY sign and through the automatic double doors, up to the check-in desk.

A young blond registration clerk shifted her gaze from the computer screen in front of her to Susan, who was gripping Keith by the arm. "May I help you?"

"Yeah, my co-worker collapsed at work. He needs to see a doctor."

The clerk handed Susan a clipboard with some forms and a pen. "Fill this out and bring it back when you're done." The clerk returned her focus to the computer screen.

Susan guided Keith to a large glass-enclosed waiting room to their left. Half of the seats were filled with patients waiting to be seen. After Keith recovered enough to fill out the patient information forms and questionnaire, Susan guided him back to the check-in desk, where a middle-aged clerk had taken over. The woman smiled, glancing at Susan's and Keith's blue-and-red Burger Barn uniforms.

"My son used to work at Burger Barn. He saved his pay and bought his first car with the money. We still go there sometimes. I like the Junior Big Barn Special the best."

Susan pursed her lips nervously and shifted her attention to Keith, who was starting to regain his strength. He had stopped blinking and stood under his own power, without swaying.

The clerk took the clipboard and scanned the forms. "Mr. Schmidt, have you been a patient at Flagler Hospital before?"

Keith answered with a soft but clear voice. "No, ma'am."

The clerk looked at him and then at Susan. "You're not family or related?"

"No, we're co-workers. We were working the same shift."

"Do you have any identification, Mr. Schmidt?"

Keith slowly pulled out his wallet and produced an Oregon driver's license. *This may not be a good thing to do.*

The clerk inspected it for a moment and commenced typing on a keyboard. She told them, "It'll be a moment while I get your information into the system."

Reading the forms, the clerk continued typing, and then stopped. "It says here your address is in Portland, Oregon. Do you have a local address?"

"I'm staying with some friends right now, until I find a place. You can use the address of Burger Barn."

Susan's eyes opened wide and she crossed her arms.

"Mr. Schmidt, do you have insurance?"

Keith mumbled, "I'm not sure. I've only been working a couple of months." He shot a nervous glance at Susan. *Why don't I know the answers to these questions?*

"He will," Susan said. "He's full-time and still working on getting his paperwork done." Susan hoped the answer was believable, though she doubted he would be covered by health insurance.

The clerk squinted and turned her head slightly to the right, and then sighed. "All right, I'll make sure you're seen by a doctor." She handed him a clipboard with more forms on it. "Fill out what you can, and we'll get you back for an exam."

***

Ben stepped out of the Flagler Hospital's second-floor elevator and strode through the large and nicely appointed waiting lounge, where families sat in upholstered chairs and couches while watching flat-screen TVs and talking among themselves.

He passed the nurses' station and found Julie Williams' private room. Tim's niece was in her bed, alone in the room. Ben went quietly to Julie's bedside and pulled up a chair. He watched the young cancer patient sleep.

After several minutes, Julie turned toward Ben and opened her eyes. "Hi, Grandpa Ben," she said softly.

Although Ben was not a blood relative, Tim and Liz had found it easier to refer to him as Grandpa, rather than explain to Julie his family connection through Uncle Tim's marriage to Ben's daughter Ruth. Ben loved the honorary title of affection and had quickly bonded with the little girl. More than making a hospital visit on this occasion, though, Ben was on a mission.

Dan's right. Christ sent me back for a reason. All of us believers are on a mission. I know he has given us the power to heal others, if we'll only use it.

"I'm going to pray for you, darling," Ben said as he held on to her arm lightly and closed his eyes.

Julie nodded. "Uncle Tim prays for me every time he comes. It makes me feel better."

Here goes. "Lord Jesus Christ, by your stripes, we are healed. I release your healing power into this young child's body. In Jesus' name, I command all cancer cells to die and all healthy cells to multiply and take their place. I command the spirit of sickness and the spirit of death to leave now, in the name of Jesus Christ, and in his name, I declare this child, Julie, healed. Amen."

Ben sensed a warmness in his hands that seemed to grow. He retained his gentle hold of Julie's arm until he felt the heat subside. He opened his eyes and stood, leaning over to give Julie a kiss on the forehead. When he straightened up, he saw that Liz had come into the room.

"Oh, hi, Ben. Surprised to see you here."

"Yeah, my visit is long overdue. Tim has been asking me to stop by, so I thought now would be a good time, while everyone was at work. I was supposed to meet Dan Lucas here, but since I arrived early and got to spend some time with Julie, I'll go downstairs and wait for him in the lobby. You take care now."

***

A man in his early forties wearing a white medical coat opened the door to the small exam room and came in with a chart in his right hand. The man glanced at Keith sitting on the exam table and looked back at the chart.

"I'm Dr. Horst. What seems to be the problem, Mr. Schmidt?"

"I have a bad headache. My co-worker says I fainted."

Dr. Horst shined an exam light into Keith's eyes and watched them begin to shift back and forth. Keith flinched and squirmed as the doctor moved the light from eye to eye. When the doctor held Keith's wrist to take his pulse, he felt scar tissue. He looked down at the wrist and then slid Keith's uniform sleeve up and saw the other scarring.

"Where are you from, Mr. Schmidt?"

"Oregon."

"Did you move out here with your family?"

"No, sir."

"You traveled across the country on your own?"

"Yes, sir."

"Your record says you're eighteen. What brings you to St. Augustine?"

"I have family in the area."

"You're not living with them?"

"Ah, not yet, sir."

The doctor turned to shine the exam light into Keith's right ear, and the light's beam caught the birthmark on Keith's neck. Dr. Horst shined the light on it before examining the ear.

"I'll be right back, Mr. Schmidt."

Dr. Horst closed the door to the exam room and slipped into an unoccupied office. Checking his watch, he closed the door and placed a call on his cell phone.

"Dr. Garvin," the voice on the phone stated.

"I think the person you're looking for is in one of our exam rooms here in the ER. He came in about an hour ago, complaining of fainting and headaches. His name is Keith Schmidt and he has a heart-shaped birthmark on the right side of his neck. He sounds like the one. You have privileges here, don't you?"

"Of course I do. Don't let him leave, no matter what you have to do. I can be there in forty-five minutes."

"All right, I'll stall, but hurry. If I drag out his exam too long, the nurses will get suspicious."

"Did he come in alone?"

"I think someone brought him in. Looks like a girlfriend."

"That's all? Not a problem. Keep him there, understand?"

At the nurses' station, the doctor instructed the charge nurse to leave the patient in exam room seven while he went to confer with a colleague.

"I may want to do an MRI, but I want to have him examined by an ENT first. Dr. Garvin will be taking him as a patient. Mr. Schmidt is stable and won't require admission at this time."

The nurse raised her eyebrows and then shrugged. "Okay. Is Dr. Garvin coming in now?"

"Yes, he's on his way."

The nurse frowned and walked away.

***

Keith woke from a shallow sleep when the door to the exam room opened. Dr. Horst returned with a man in a dark shirt covered by a white coat.

"Mr. Schmidt, this is Dr. Garvin. He's an ear, nose, and throat specialist I've called in to consult on your case. He'll examine you now." Dr. Horst turned and left the room.

Dr. Garvin kept his hands in his lab coat and stared straight at Keith. Keith sensed evil, but fought his danger instinct. Dr. Garvin moved closer and removed his left hand from his coat. He held an exam light.

"All right, Mr. Schmidt. I understand you fainted and have a headache. Let's take a look."

Keith's sense of foreboding grew. The tone of the doctor's voice and his mannerisms reminded him of some of his father's associates.

"Yeah, but I think I'm getting better now." Keith felt the urge to run.

Dr. Garvin gave him a terse stare. "Now, you never know how these things start and what they can lead to. We can't be too careful when fainting is involved. Could be an inner ear infection or something much more serious."

The doctor shined his exam light in Keith's left nostril. "Head back, please. Let's take a peek through the looking glass and see who's in there."

Keith jerked his body back on the table. He recognized the term *looking glass* from his years of abuse. *He's trying to trigger me.*

Instantly, the young man re-experienced the shock of an electric cattle prod. He lurched forward and caught the doctor under the chin with his left shoulder. The blow lifted the doctor and caused an amulet the doctor was wearing around his neck to fly out from under his shirt. Keith recognized the pentagram with the goat head symbol.

He pushed away from the startled doctor, who had reached into his coat and pulled out a hypodermic needle still in a safety cap.

"End of the line for you, Keith. Time to go to never-never land. When you disobey orders, you pay. You know that."

The doctor pulled the cap off the needle and thrust it toward Keith's neck. Keith parried the doctor's arm with his left forearm and pushed the smaller man to the floor. The doctor knocked over a small exam table as he fell.

Keith jerked the exam room door open and ran into the waiting room, where he startled Susan, who was checking her phone.

"Susan, we need to get out of here. Now!"

Keith grabbed her by the arm and nearly pulled her off her feet as his defensive subpersonality took control. They sprinted toward the front door.

***

Finally, Dan Lucas found a parking spot in the last row of the east side of Flagler Hospital's north parking lot, one that met his requirements. He wanted a space on the end to reduce the chance of another car door marring his cherished Dodge Charger's flawless paint. His driving around to find the perfect spot had cost him valuable time. He checked his watch. *Three fifteen. I'm late. Hope Ben's still here.*

Dan locked his car and hurried to make up for lost time. Heading toward the main northern entrance, he took a shortcut in front of the emergency room. While he strode under the awning that covered the emergency room's automatic sliding glass door, a young man burst from the ER entrance and nearly knocked him over.

The attending nurse was running after Keith, yelling, "Mr. Schmidt, Mr. Schmidt, where are you going? The doctor hasn't finished your exam."

Dan caught a glimpse of a wine-colored birthmark on the teen's neck. The name "Schmidt" pierced Dan's thoughts like an electric shock.

Oh my God, it's him! He turned instinctively and yelled, "Your real father, Ben, is in Palm Coast at the Radiant Love Church."

206

Keith turned his head for a second in Dan's direction, and kept running with Susan in tow until they had vanished from Dan's view.

Dan turned around and saw a doctor running out of the ER entrance while cradling a hypodermic needle in his right hand that was partially concealed by his lab coat.

Instinctively, Dan stepped to his left and caught the doctor with a left elbow strike to the chin and then pretended to stumble in an attempt to feign being pushed by the doctor.

Dr. Garvin fell from the force of the blow. Dan's smooth actions and split-second timing made the encounter appear to be an honest collision caused by the pursuing doctor.

Several nurses rushed to attend to Dr. Garvin, and Dr. Horst ran toward his colleague, but stopped when he saw the crowd gathering around his fallen colleague and Dan. He stood for a few seconds, and then slowly turned and went back into the ER.

Dr. Garvin, after starting to regain his senses, stared up at Dan and yelled, "You idiot. I'm going to have you arrested."

"Oh, I'm so sorry, Doctor, I didn't see you coming."

The attending nurses stared in shock at Dr. Garvin, still lying on the pavement, and after Dan declared his sincere apologies, they all knowingly nodded, and he excused himself. When he stepped away from the crowd, Dan shifted into full operational mode as Dr. Garvin got up, brushed himself off, and proceeded toward the parking lot while the shocked ER staff watched.

Dan paused, pretending to gather himself and recover from the "accident" while he kept his eyes locked on the retreating Dr. Garvin, who was now moving at a much faster pace.

After the emergency room staff, in a state of confusion, began to make their way back into the hospital, Dan launched into a pursuit of the fleeing doctor. His instincts told him what he needed to do. Careful to use parked cars as cover, Dan shadowed Dr. Garvin and watched him stride hurriedly to the visiting physicians' parking lot while scanning the rows of cars for Keith or his vehicle.

When he failed to find Keith, he turned and got into his black Range Rover. Dan shielded himself from view behind a car and took photos with his cell phone, of Garvin stopping his SUV momentarily after backing out of his parking spot and shifting into drive.

"Got ya!" Dan said, and confirmed the clarity of several shots of Garvin's license plate.

With a grin on his face, Dan turned and headed into Flagler's main entrance and stopped to sit in the lobby. After pausing to reflect on what had just happened, he scanned his photos for the clearest shot of Garvin's license plate. He texted it to Detective Charlie Walker, with a note.

"Run this tag. May be a lead in your child homicide case. I'll call later and explain. Dan."

He put his phone away and went toward the elevators, when he remembered he'd forgotten to meet Ben in Julie's hospital room. Quickening his pace, he caught a glimpse of Ben standing near the bank of elevators.

"Man, I'm sorry I'm so late. What are you doing here? I thought you were going to be upstairs," Dan said.

"I took your advice and did what I had to do with Julie. I know my authority and where it comes from. You were right. It's not so difficult to declare healing. It's not my power, its Christ's."

Ben took a step backward and eyed Dan from head to toe, surprised by his disheveled—something unheard of—appearance. "What happened to you? Are you okay?"

"Yeah, I'm fine." Dan straightened his shirt and smoothed his hair. Then he stopped and nearly froze when he mentally reran what had happened outside. *Good grief!* He turned to Ben. "I think I saw your son Keith leaving the ER a few minutes ago."

Chapter 20
Closure

Almost time. Dan checked the time and peered nervously into the sanctuary of the Radiant Love Church. From his vantage point by the side of the main church entrance, he watched a husband and wife hand out church bulletins and warmly greet the steady stream of people slowly making their way into the church. The rows of seats were beginning to fill. *Almost time for the ten o'clock Sunday worship service to start.* Dan took some deep breaths and willed the butterflies in his stomach to calm down.

I guess running the article in the paper paid off. Dan had been skeptical about putting his picture in the paper and titling the contributed article, "NCIS Special Agent Presents Evidence of Life after Death." *Nothing like the shameless promotion of your past. At least my text messages were more down to earth. Hope some of my invitees attend.*

Ben joined Dan, who was now standing along the back wall. With a tone of anxious optimism, Ben said, "You're attracting quite a crowd. Are you ready for this?"

Dan nodded slowly. "This is what we wanted, right? To reach a lot of people with the truth." Dan gave a nervous laugh. "Sometimes we have to be careful what we wish for."

Ben nodded. "I'm beginning to understand that, with this new life. But between the two of us, we'll get the job done."

Pastor Tim soon joined the two men. "You're a big draw," he said, patting Dan on the shoulder. "I don't recognize two-thirds of the people here. Looks like it'll be standing room only."

Tim indicated for them to follow him toward the chancel of the church.

"Be ready in case I need your help," Dan said in Ben's direction. *Now I'm the one with doubts.*

Ben narrowed his eyes at Dan. "This is your show, my friend. I'm only a spectator, remember?"

The three men went in single file along the side of the church while the praise band played a captivating worship song. While Dan surveyed the crowd for people he recognized, some familiar faces caught his eye. A smiling and surprisingly healthy-looking Julie Williams sat next to her mother, Liz, in a middle row. Julie's hair had grown back and was long enough to hold a purple bow. Her complexion glowed and she had regained most of her weight.

Dan stepped forward quickly and elbowed Ben, speaking in a half whisper in Ben's ear as they made their way toward the front of the nave.

"You didn't tell me Julie was getting better."

"I didn't want to distract you while you were preparing for today. Seems my little prayer in Julie's hospital room had an effect. She's not only getting better, but her cancer is in complete remission."

Ben winked as they approached the front row, where Connie Lucas and Ruth Williams were seated.

Dan sat and took Connie's hand. He gave it a squeeze and whispered, "Wish me luck."

Connie turned and whispered in his ear, "You're ready for this. Be yourself and let God do the talking."

Dan mouthed the words "I will" to Connie, who turned to watch Tim climb the carpeted steps to the classically constructed oak pulpit located on the right side of the large altar. A matching plain oak cross was mounted on the front of the podium-style structure.

After the music stopped and the congregation sat down, Tim greeted the packed house of worshippers. Every seat was taken. Ushers were busy setting up folding chairs along the back wall of the church to accommodate late arrivals.

"Good morning and welcome to Radiant Love Church," Tim announced. "We're so glad to have all of you with us here today in the Lord's house. We have a special treat for you this morning. Our message will be delivered by retired NCIS special agent Dan Lucas. Dan served around the world in many senior-level NCIS positions, for nearly three decades. He's an expert in counterintelligence, and he's tracked dangerous terrorists and fought crime his whole career. He's also the author of the brand-new book *From Death to Life*, and he has a message that should resonate with us all. Dan will be signing some advance copies in the fellowship hall after the service. Please join us then for some refreshments and to say hello to him."

Dan could feel the palms of his hands sweating and his pulse increasing. *Now's not the time for the jitters.*

"Now," Tim said, "I know you may be wondering why we have a retired law enforcement officer delivering the sermon today, but when you hear what he has to say, I think you'll agree God can use *any* one of us to present a message he wants us to hear. None of Jesus' disciples were trained clergy, yet they traveled the ancient world and taught the Gospel after Christ's death and Resurrection. If it hadn't been for their faithful work, we wouldn't be here worshiping together today. Please welcome retired NCIS special agent Dan Lucas."

Dan rose and proceeded to the pulpit as the audience's applause resonated throughout the church. *God, please give me the words you want me to say.*

"Good morning, everyone, and thank you, Pastor Williams, for the warm welcome. I take your applause as a tribute to Father God.

He's responsible for me being here today." Dan cleared his throat and adjusted the height of the microphone.

"Pastor Williams mentioned that Jesus' disciples taught the Gospel even though they were not professional clergy. All of Christ's disciples, except for Judas, were motivated by a love for Jesus and a love for their fellow man. Their devotion to Jesus, their compassion for others, and their dedication to the truth moved them to endure extreme hardships, brutal punishments, and ultimately, horrific deaths.

"I stand here today for the same reason. I have compassion for people, and my compassion drives me to try to help people understand that the Bible is truly God-inspired and full of truths. It's a book of facts, history, wisdom, prophecy, promises, and warnings."

Dan paused to allow the congregation time to digest his words.

"You know, we tend to focus exclusively on the promises of the Bible these days, and shy away from the warnings. It's not politically correct to talk about subjects that make people uncomfortable. But the Bible clearly warns us that if we die before we confess our sins and ask God to forgive us, we'll end up in hell. Period. That kind of blunt message is not welcome in most churches today, but it needs to be heard. That's why I'm here.

"As Pastor Williams said, I spent most of my NCIS career in counterintelligence. I hired on as a new agent in 1981. Years later, the 1980s became known as the decade of the spy. Why? A record number of Americans were caught during that time spying for hostile countries. Like many newly hired NCIS agents, I spent the first couple of years warning US Navy and Marine Corps commands about the threat from hostile intelligence services. To be honest, some had trouble taking my warnings seriously, since hostile intelligence officers conceal their identities and operate in secret. I was warning them about a threat they couldn't see, so some tuned me out. Others realized many years later that they should have heeded my warnings. Today we've all heard about the threat from foreign spies who've targeted our country.

"I'm still warning people about a danger you can't see, but this time it's a different kind of threat. Today I'm motivated by more than patriotism and a call to duty. I'm motivated by compassion and love. You know love can be expressed in many ways. The love I offer you comes in the form of a warning.

"When Jesus Christ walked the earth nearly two thousand years ago, he taught his disciples and anyone who'd listen to him some profound truths. Some of his truths were his promises of bliss for eternity ... for anyone who would believe he was God in the flesh and would try their best to obey his commands. But intermixed in his teachings were warnings about what would happen to anyone who ignored his declarations about eternity. Jesus made it clear that if we reject his forewarning about the consequences of turning our backs on God and dying before we repent of our sins, we'd suffer for eternity in ways we could never comprehend.

"We all know the Scriptures describe how Jesus Christ was executed. We know that the Bible documents Jesus making the ultimate sacrifice by giving his physical life to save us. But have you ever stopped to think about what exactly Jesus was saving us from?"

Dan paused and studied the faces of some in the crowd. He noticed Connie's warm gaze of approval and encouragement.

"The question is vitally important, since you won't hear it asked in many churches today. It bothers people, but it must be asked. Why would God have his only son die a slow, agonizing death by torture, if we all end up in heaven, anyway? Or, why would he have Jesus suffer through such a horrific experience if, once we take our last breath, everything goes dark and our lives are over? And why did Jesus agree to be subjected to such a grizzly execution?

"For over thirty years of my life, I spent many hours identifying, gathering, and analyzing evidence. Some of the evidence was physical trace evidence from crime scenes, some was documentation from white-collar crime cases, and much of it was information that came from informants and recruited sources and assets who had secrets about our adversaries that they were prepared to share. I learned how to distinguish between fabrication and fact and what signs to look for when I was trying to determine whether a person was telling the truth. In every case, I never accepted anything I was told at face value. I always tried to find a way to confirm or refute the truthfulness of the information I obtained."

Dan stopped for a moment. "I was also always careful about how I handled evidence and sensitive information. Yet, in other areas in my life, I was careless. Unlike many of you in this church, I wasn't always a faithful follower of Christ. I was a cultural Christian who intellectually accepted the premise that a supreme Creator existed, but I saw no relevance in a belief system that had no visible effect on my daily life. It wasn't until I first read about people who had visited heaven and hell during out-of-body experiences and near-death experiences that I started to consider that the things I couldn't see were more important than the things I could see. Sound crazy? Not biblical?"

Dan paused to allow the audience to ponder his point.

"The apostle Paul reports, in 1 Corinthians 12:2, that he visited heaven, but did not know whether he was in his body or out of his body at the time of his travel. When I saw Scripture that confirmed out-of-body experiences actually happen, I was surprised. As I dug deeper, I discovered that some of the books about out-of-body experiences and near-death experiences contained eyewitness accounts reported in a way that truthful witnesses would normally report information. That got my attention. When I realized some of the books were probably true, I went to work and dug through the research of others. My multi-year investigative process has brought me here today. My book, *From Death to Life*, is the result. The book is actually a report of my investigation about what happens after we take our last breath."

Dan stopped and scanned the audience to gauge their attention level. Most eyes were fixed on him. While he looked down to turn the page of his notes, two late arrivals entered the church and quickly took seats along the back wall.

"When you stop and think about it, we are all terminal cases. The only question is *when* we will take our last breath."

Dan glanced at Connie, who smiled and nodded.

"Scripture tells us man is appointed to die once, but when is that? We all know modern medicine can resuscitate people whose hearts have stopped beating. We may think a person has reached their appointed time to die, but God knows differently. God has his own timing, and one thing you can be sure of, God is always on time in anything he does, since he's the author of time. He may want to delay their death and turn their misfortune into an opportunity. An opportunity for God to send them on a special mission."

Dan paused and glanced at his notes.

"Pastor Williams introduced me as a retired special agent. What does the title special agent actually mean? It's a title for people who want to serve their country in an official capacity. For example, NCIS special agents are individuals who've met certain eligibility requirements, have been administered an oath, and are appointed as civilian agents of the US government to carry out official missions and enforce federal laws. But beyond the dry technical description, special agents are people who sometimes get called upon to reach deep into their souls and give everything they have to serve others, including their lives. 'Serve those who protect and protect those who serve' is their motto."

Dan hesitated and surveyed the crowd. "God has his own special agents. And he chooses them for special missions, too. God chose Dr. Ben Chernick to perform a special mission—a mission borne out of Ben's unfathomable depths of despair and unspeakable suffering. A mission precipitated by Ben's clinical death and his terrifying descent into hell. When he was near physical annihilation,

Ben called out to Jesus Christ to save him, and Christ answered with mercy and love. During his rescue of Ben, Christ directed Ben to tell the world what he'd experienced. But Ben's mission is more than confirming the existence of a dominion of demons and unquenchable fire. It's a mission to declare God's compassion and love for all. A love that drives God to use every possible means to warn his creation of the perils they face if they choose to go through life without him. When I met Ben last year, he would have been the last person I would have ever chosen to go on a mission for God. Now I'm here to tell you he's the first."

The crowd stirred and whispers became audible. Ben frowned and sank down in his seat. Dan instantly regretted bringing up Ben's experience, but then a strange calm came over the retired agent. He glanced down at his notes to collect his thoughts while the congregation quieted.

"God's recruitment of Ben for his mission began with three near-death experiences. Some of you may be skeptical. You should be aware that scientists, physicians, academics, and researchers have studied the phenomenon of near-death experiences for more than four decades. The cumulative results of their research include the finding that roughly five percent of the world's population has undergone some form of a near-death experience. The question is not *if* they're happening, but *how* and *why*. Especially for us here today, what are the ramifications for followers of Christ? I try to answer those questions in my book. You can be the judge of whether I've succeeded or not."

Ben gave Dan a look of relief and slowly nodded his head while smiling.

"That brings me to the second question I raised. Why did he do it? Why did Jesus allow himself to be brutally executed? He could have called down legions of angels to rescue him and he could return to a wonderful life in heaven. Yes, we would all go to hell if he had chosen to skip his crucifixion, but he could have justified his escape by pointing to the complete and total betrayal of him by many in Jerusalem. Instead, he died for us anyway. And that raises the most important question. What did we do to make him love us? The answer is nothing. I didn't do a thing and neither did any of you. He laid down his life because he loved us. All he asks is for our love in return. That's the definition of grace."

Ben jumped to his feet and bounded up the altar steps to the pulpit. Dan stopped before his next sentence and stared at Ben in shock. Ben stood next to Dan at the podium and grinned, and a surprised Dan stepped to the side.

"Sorry to interrupt you, my good friend, but it's time for me to take a stand," Ben said under his breath while he lowered the microphone.

"Ladies and gentlemen, pardon my interruption of Mr. Lucas, but I felt compelled to make a few remarks since I can confirm that what he has been telling you is the truth. I did go to hell. I wasn't a believer at the time, but I am now."

The congregation murmured among themselves while Ben surveyed them. The room became quiet. Dan stood to the right of the pulpit, with his hands clasped behind him.

"I know what I'm saying is shocking to some," Ben said, "but we shouldn't be surprised to hear that hell actually exists. After all, Jesus spoke more about hell than heaven while he walked this earth. I believe he did so for a reason. He knew his words would be captured in writing and placed in the Bible, to stand as a warning for every generation to come. He didn't want anyone to have a false sense of security. He even warned us that many would take the broad road to destruction while few would take the narrow path to life. I was on that wide path and oblivious to where I was headed. I thought hell was merely a mythical construct conjured up by our ancient ancestors to scare us into compliance. I don't think that anymore. It's a literal place where many, I'm sad to say, end up. I know ... I saw many poor souls there during my visits."

All eyes were glued on him.

"As Dan said, God selected me to be one of his special agents. My mission is to warn others that hell is real. If you don't remember anything else you heard this morning, please remember this: We must have a relationship with Jesus Christ in order to stay out of hell, that place of eternal torment. My message is not a scare tactic, it's a warning that I share from the bottom of my heart."

Ben paused and composed himself. "My message wouldn't be complete, though, if I didn't make clear the most important lesson I learned during my ordeal. God loves us more than anyone can imagine. When I called out to Jesus Christ to rescue me from a lake of burning grease, he reached down and pulled me out without asking me any questions, without asking me to show my loyalty to him or do anything else. He rescued me like a true hero because he loves me. He loves you too. Call on him in prayer and get to know him. You won't regret it. Take it from someone who had to learn the hard way. God is real, and so are heaven and hell. Thank you."

While Ben left the podium and returned to his seat, Dan stepped to the microphone.

"Thank you, Ben, for your heartfelt testimony. It took courage to come up here and tell the truth." He paused. "Ben will be in the fellowship hall with me, if you want to ask him any questions. … In closing, I hope all of you take the time to carefully consider what Ben and I shared with you today. The stakes couldn't be higher for you, your children, for all those you love. Thank you, ladies and gentlemen, and God bless."

The congregation rose to their feet and greeted Dan with thunderous applause as he returned to his seat and sat next to Connie. They faced each other, motionless for a moment. Connie gave Dan a loving hug.

After the extended applause ended, the worship leader led the congregation in a final song. Pastor Williams then rose and, after thanking both Dan and Ben, gave the benediction and dismissed the worshipers. Connie and Ruth remained in the worship room to talk with friends while Dan and Ben headed to the fellowship hall.

***

"I hope I helped your presentation," Ben said with a sheepish grin as he and Dan walked through the breezeway. "Sorry for barging in like that during the middle of your message. I couldn't help myself."

"Are you kidding me? You *made* my presentation. See how we need to work together to get the message out?"

Piles of Dan's book were stacked on a long table in the fellowship hall, next to a large poster with a color photo of the book cover and the caption, *Time to Learn the Truth. Read and Believe.* A local publishing company had done a limited printing of a prepublication version of his book in time for Dan's presentation.

Dan went behind the display table to straighten and reposition the stacks of books that had been disturbed when someone had moved the table during the church service. While Dan was hurriedly trying to bring order to the display, a stylishly-dressed middle-aged brunette approached the table and extended her hand.

"I'm Denise Anderson, with Lerner and Steele Publishing. I got your text message, Mr. Lucas. I thought this trip would be a good excuse for a Florida vacation, but a few minutes ago I listened to our newest author. Your message was spot on. You're a natural communicator, and if you use your gift like you did today, you'll attract readers. I was the one who killed your contract, Mr. Lucas. I didn't think you'd be able to rise above a crowded field of writers and make your voice heard, but I see I was wrong. You have what it takes to be a successful writer and speaker. We also might be interested in Dr. Chernick's story. He'd be a great subject for a follow-on book."

"I'm glad you came," Dan said, elated she'd received his text message. "I understand about the contract. I know I was a little reluctant to start a speaking program, but you were right. I do need to get out and make myself known, and that includes talking about my former profession. Thanks for taking the time to make the trip down and giving me a second look."

"It was my pleasure, Mr. Lucas. I'm the one who's glad I gave you a second look. I almost let a talented author get away. By the way, your advance copies turned out nice, but when our graphics department redoes your cover, you'll be impressed. I'll be in touch. Expect a contract in the mail in two weeks. Welcome aboard, Mr. Lucas."

Dan grinned from ear to ear. He turned to see if Ben had heard any of the conversation, but it appeared he hadn't. Ben was still busy, with his back to them, adjusting the position of the chairs behind the display table. By the time he'd turned in Dan's direction, Ms. Anderson had left.

While Ben straightened the last chair, he felt a hand tap his shoulder. Assuming it was Dan, he spoke without turning. "I need to tidy things up a bit and make sure your table looks presentable," Ben said in Dan's direction. "You're about to become a published author now and you need to have a professional image, particularly if I'm going to be your partner."

Ben felt a second tap and then the clear voice of a young man: "I'm Keith Schmidt. Are you my father?"

Ben spun around and found a young man in casual clothes standing with his arms at his sides. Instantly, Ben recognized the dark hair and olive complexion as his own. Within seconds, his eyes trained on the wine-colored birthmark on his neck. A tidal wave of joy swept over Ben and washed him with ecstasy. *It's my son and he wants me to be his father. Yes, yes, yes!*

"Yes, I'm your father," he managed to reply around the large lump in his throat.

Ben embraced Keith with a strong bear hug. Tears streamed down Ben's face and he said, "Thank God I found you! You're alive! I was so afraid of what might have happened to you."

Keith held onto Ben as tightly as Ben held him. "Yes, Dad, I'm alive."

Dan beamed. He stood at a distance and watched the scene unfold. He knew God was at work in this unbelievable moment. He also knew God had bigger plans for him in the future. He didn't know how God could top this, but he was certain he'd find out.

Evidence for Eternity

Do you feel you have too many choices in life when it comes to deciding what to believe about God and the possibility of an afterlife? Can't decide what to do and worried that you'll make the wrong choice?

I've been in your shoes, and my intense desire to find the truth about life, death, and beyond, drove me to write *Final Departure* and to follow up with *Divine Return*. Both novels contain facts that I've developed after years of study.

I strive to serve as a credible resource for those who seek the truth about some of the minefield subjects that most churches ignore today. I try to address complex faith-related questions in a logical, straightforward way, with a wake-up call emphasis.

I believe I'm currently the only NCIS special agent veteran—or any national security community old hand, for that matter—who is lending his or her skills to spotlight the truth about evidence for eternity.

Yes, evidence proves that we do go on to exist for eternity after physically dying, but it's often hidden, obscured, or reported in a deceptive way to keep you in the dark.

The evidence will convince you that God and his Kingdom exist.

I want to share with you what I've learned.

I spent years protecting our country, and now I'm serving as an advocate to preserve the truth about God.

Please join me on my journey to seek out and spotlight the truth.

Learn more at **www.evidenceforeternity.com**.

About the Author

Jeff Walton, an award-winning author and communicator, is a US Navy Vietnam veteran and retired US Naval Criminal Investigative Service (NCIS) special agent who spent more than thirty-four years in federal law enforcement and national security work.

His career assignments ranged from felony criminal investigations to counterintelligence and combating terrorism operations and investigations in the United States, the Far East, and Europe.

He also served in senior management positions at NCIS Headquarters, the Office of the Assistant Secretary of Defense for C3I, the National Counterintelligence Center, and the Office of the National Counterintelligence Executive.

He and his wife live in Florida.

Thank you for reading my book.

I hope you found *Divine Return* to be both entertaining and stimulating. I learned a great deal during the research phase of the book. I am neither a Bible scholar nor a clergyman; I'm simply a student of the Bible.

I have assembled information I believe will help you to better grasp some of the key areas of research and commentary that a relatively small group of Christian scholars continue to focus on in search of the truth.

I wrote *Divine Return* to serve as a starting point for your own study and research.

If you enjoyed the book, please do me the great favor of writing a review. You can do so at any of the popular online booksellers.

Please share your thoughts with me. You can contact me at **jeffwaltonbooks@gmail.com.**

Sincerely,

Jeff Walton

Ordering Information

Final Departure
by Jeff Walton
ISBN: 978-0-9974334-0-1

Divine Return
Death Is Never The End
ISBN: 978-0-9974334-3-2

Sunbrook Publishing
PO Box 730
St. Augustine, FL 32085
www.JeffWaltonBooks.com
JeffWaltonBooks@gmail.com

Printed in Great Britain
by Amazon